Belgian by n... Kobe, Japan, and currently lives in Paris. She is the bestselling author of fifteen novels, translated into thirty languages. *Fear and Trembling* won the Grand Prix of the Académie Française and the Prix Internet du Livre, and her UK debut, *The Book of Proper Names*, was published by Faber in 2004.

The Character of Rain
'Concise, philosophical, enigmatic, her writing is highly personal and beyond fault . . . it is a belated treat that her books are finally being published in the UK.' *Guardian*

The Book of Proper Names
'This prose clear as chilled chablis that you savour by the syllable, and want to start again the moment the book finished.' *The Times*

Antichrista
'Her wit is so dry [and] her intelligence is unnerving. She creates a very personal world, but few are more rewarding.' *Independent on Sunday*

Loving Sabotage
'Stunningly original . . . The portrayal of ensuing loss of childhood innocence is both fiercely comic and painfully cruel.' *Observer*

The Life of Hunger will be published by Faber in summer 2006.

Fear and Trembling

AMÉLIE NOTHOMB

Translated from the French by Adriana Hunter

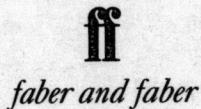

faber and faber

First published in France under the title *Stupeur et tremblements*
in 1999 by Editions Albin Michel S. A.

First published in the United States in 2002 by St Martin's Griffin

First published in Great Britain
in 2004 by Faber and Faber Limited
3 Queen Square London WCIN 3AU
This edition published in 2006

Printed in England by Mackays of Chatham Ltd, Chatham, Kent

A CIP record for this book
is available from the British Library

ISBN 0–571–23389–9
ISBN 978–0–571–23389–2

2 4 6 8 10 9 7 5 3 1

FEAR AND TREMBLING

MISTER HANEDA WAS senior to Mister Omochi, who was senior to Mister Saito, who was senior to Miss Mori, who was senior to me. I was senior to no one.

You could put this another way. I took orders from Miss Mori, who took orders from Mister Saito, and so on up the ladder; of course, orders that came down could jump a level or two.

And so it was that, within the import-export division of the Yumimoto Corporation, I took orders from everyone.

ON THE 8th of January in 1990 an elevator spat me out on the top floor of a towering Tokyo office building. An enormous bay window at the far end of the landing sucked me over with the irresistible force of a shattered porthole on an airplane. Far, very far, below, I could see the city; it seemed so distant and unreal from that height that suddenly I wasn't sure I had ever even set foot there.

It didn't occur to me that I ought to introduce myself at the reception desk. Actually, at that moment, I didn't have a single thought in my head, nothing aside from fascination with the endless space outside the great bay window.

Eventually a hoarse voice from behind pronounced my name. I turned around. A small, thin, ugly man in his fifties was looking at me irritably.

"Why didn't you let the receptionist know that you'd arrived?" he asked.

I couldn't think of anything to say. I bowed my head and shoulders, realizing that in just ten minutes, and without having spoken a single word, I had made a bad impression on my first day at Yumimoto.

The man told me he was Mister Saito. He led me through huge, endless, open-plan offices, introducing me to hordes of people whose names I forgot as soon as he had pronounced them.

He showed me the office that was the domain of his superior, Mister Omochi, who was enormously fat and terrifying, proving that he was the vice-president of the division.

Then he indicated a door and announced solemnly that behind it was Mister Haneda, the president. It went without saying that I shouldn't even dream of meeting him.

Finally he led me to a gigantic office in which at least forty people were working. He indicated a desk, which sat directly opposite from another desk, belonging, he informed me, to my immediate superior, Miss Mori. She was in a meeting and would join me in the early afternoon.

Mister Saito introduced me briefly to the assembly, after which he asked me whether I enjoyed a challenge. It was clear saying no would not be an option.

"Yes," I said.

It was the first word I had spoken. Until then, I had made do with tilting my head.

The "challenge" that Mister Saito was proposing consisted of accepting an invitation on his behalf from someone named Adam Johnson, to play golf the following Sunday. I was to write a letter of acceptance to this gentleman in English.

"Who is Adam Johnson?" I was stupid enough to ask.

My superior sighed exasperatedly and didn't answer. I wondered whether it was absurd not to know who Mister Johnson was. Was my question indiscreet? I never found out, nor ever learned who Adam Johnson was.

The exercise seemed simple enough. I sat down and wrote a cordial letter, something along the lines of "Mister Saito would be delighted to play golf next Sunday with Mister Johnson, and sends him his best regards, etc, etc." I took it to Mister Saito.

He read my work, gave a scornful little cry, and tore it up.

"Start over."

I thought I had perhaps been too friendly or familiar with Adam Johnson, and composed a cold, formal reply. "Mister Saito acknowledges Mister Johnson's request and wishes to inform him of his willingness to conform with his desires by engaging in a game of golf with him, etc, etc."

He read my work, gave a scornful little cry, and tore it up.

"Start over."

I wanted to ask what I had done wrong, but it was clear Mister Saito did not tolerate questions, as had been proved by his reaction to my brief inquiry into the identity of the letter's recipient. I would, therefore, have to find for myself the correct phraseology with which to address this mysterious golfer, Adam Johnson.

I spent the next few hours composing missives. Mister Saito punctuated my output by tearing it up, with no other commentary than that same little cry; it became a sort of refrain. Each time I had to come up with a new formula.

There was something "Fair duchess, I am dying of love for you" about this whole exercise that demanded a certain amount of creative wit. I explored permutations of grammatical categories. What if "Adam Johnson" were the verb, "next Sunday" the subject, "playing golf" the object, and "Mister Saito" the adverb? "Next Sunday accepts with pleasure the invitation to go Adamjohnsoning a playing golf MisterSaitoingly." Take that, Aristotle!

I was just beginning to enjoy myself when Mister Saito interrupted me. He tore up the umpteenth letter without even reading it and told me that Miss Mori had arrived.

"You will work with her this afternoon. In the meantime, go and get me a cup of coffee."

It was already two o'clock in the afternoon. My epistolary exercises had so absorbed me that I had forgotten about taking a break.

I put the cup down on Mister Saito's desk and turned around. A young woman as tall and slender as an archer's bow was walking toward me.

Whenever I think of Fubuki Mori, I see the Japanese longbow, taller than a man. That's why I have decided to call the company "Yumimoto," which means "pertaining to the bow."

And whenever I see a bow, I think of Fubuki.

"MISS MORI?"

"Please, call me Fubuki."

5

Miss Mori was at least five feet ten, a height few Japanese men achieved. She was ravishingly svelte and graceful despite the stiffness to which she, like all Japanese women, had to sacrifice herself. But what transfixed me was the splendor of her face.

She was talking to me. The sound of her soft voice brimmed with intelligence. She was showing me some files, explaining what they contained, and smiling. I was dimly aware that I wasn't listening to what she was saying.

Then she invited me to read the documents she had placed on my desk, which, as I've said, was opposite hers. She sat down and started to work. I leafed meekly through the paperwork. It dealt with rulings and listings.

The spectacle of her face, a mere eight feet away, was captivating. Her eyelids were lowered over some pages with numbers, so she couldn't see that I was studying her closely. She had the most beautiful nose in the world, a Japanese nose, an inimitable nose, whose delicate nostrils would be recognized among a thousand others. Not all Japanese have this nose, but anyone who has can only be of Japanese descent. Had Cleopatra had this nose, the history and geography of the world would have undergone a major shift.

———

THAT EVENING, AFTER I'd gotten home, it would have been petty to have thought that none of the abilities for which I had assumed I had been hired by Yumimoto had been put to any use. I had wanted to work in a Japanese company. And that's what I was doing. I felt it had been an excellent day. The next few days confirmed that feeling.

I still didn't quite know what my job was; I didn't care. Mister Saito seemed somehow dismayed by my letter-writing skills; I didn't care. I was too enchanted by my colleague, my superior, Miss Mori, whose friendship alone provided ample reason to spend ten hours a day working in an office.

Her complexion, simultaneously white and dusky, was of the kind the poet Tanizaki describes so beautifully. Fubuki was the incarnation of Japanese beauty—with the stupefying exception of her height. Her face suggested a direct connection to the *nadeshiko* (carnation), a nostalgic symbol of the young Japanese virgin in former times. Perched on her towering silhouette, it was designed to rule the world.

YUMIMOTO WAS ONE of the largest corporations in the Japanese business universe. The Import-Export

Division, as far as I could tell, bought and sold everything on the face of the entire planet.

Yumimoto's import-export catalog was truly titanic: from Finnish Emmental to Singaporean soda, by way of Canadian optical fibers, French tires, and Togoan jute. Nothing escaped its grasp.

The money involved exceeded human comprehension. After a given accumulation of zeroes, the sums left the realm of recognizable numbers and entered into that of abstract art. I wondered whether in the heart of this company lived some creature that rejoiced at making a hundred million yen, or mourned losing an equivalent amount.

Yumimoto's employees, like these zeroes, were of value only in relation to the other employees. All, that is, except me, who didn't even have the value of a zero.

The days passed and I still didn't have anything much to do. I was not greatly bothered by this. Being forgotten was not an unpleasant feeling. I sat at my desk, reading and re-reading the documents Fubuki had given me. They were prodigiously uninteresting, with the exception of one, which listed all Import-Export employees—their last names, first names, dates and places of birth, names of spouse if they had one, and of their children, with dates of birth.

There was nothing fascinating about these facts in and

of themselves. But when you are very hungry the tiniest crust of bread is a feast. In the starved state in which my brain found itself, the list seemed as juicy as a gossip magazine. It was also the only document that I understood.

To appear as if I were working, I decided to memorize the list by heart. There were about a hundred names. Most employees were married with children; this made my task more of a challenge.

I worked at it, bending my head over the material, then raising it so that I could commit it all to memory. When I looked up, my gaze always landed on Fubuki's face opposite me.

MISTER SAITO STOPPED asking me to write letters to Adam Johnson—or to anyone else. He didn't ask me to do anything, actually, except bring him cups of coffee.

Nothing could be more normal when beginning a career in a Japanese company than starting with the *ôchakumi*—"the honorable function of making tea." I took this role all the more seriously because it was the only one I had.

I soon knew everyone's drinking habits: for Mister Saito, a cup of black coffee at exactly eight-thirty; for Mister Unaji, regular coffee with two spoonfuls of sugar at ten o'clock; for Mister Mizuno, a mug of cocoa on the hour; for Mister Okada, a cup of English tea with a hint of cloud of milk at five o'clock; and for Fubuki, a cup of green tea at nine o'clock, black coffee at noon, a second cup of green tea at three, and a last cup of black coffee at five. She thanked me each time with charming courtesy.

THIS HUMBLE TASK turned out to be the first instrument of my downfall at Yumimoto.

One morning, Mister Saito informed me that the vice-president was receiving an important delegation from a sister company in his office.

"Coffee for twenty people."

I entered Mister Omochi's office carrying a large tray, and performed to perfection. I served each cup with studied humility, incanting the most refined phrases in current usage, lowering my eyes, and bowing. If there were such a thing as an *ōchakumi* Order of Merit, it would have been awarded to me.

The delegation left several hours later. The voice of the enormously fat Mister Omochi thundered.

"SAITO-SAN!"

Mister Saito leaped to his feet, turned white, and trotted into the vice-president's lair. The Obese One's bellowings reverberated on the other side of the wall. I couldn't make out what he was saying, but it didn't sound like anything pleasant.

Mister Saito returned, his face ashen. I felt a rush of tenderness for him, thinking that the poor man was only a third the weight of his aggressor. He called for me, furiously.

I followed him to an empty office. His anger made him stammer.

"You have thoroughly antagonized the delegation from our sister company! You served the coffee using phrases that suggested you speak Japanese absolutely perfectly!"

"I don't speak it all that badly, Saito-san."

"Be quiet! Why do you believe you can defend yourself? Mister Omochi is very angry. You created the most appalling tension in the meeting this morning. How could our business partners have any feeling of trust in the presence of a white girl who understood their language? From now on you will no longer speak Japanese."

I was dumbfounded.

"I beg your pardon?"

"You no longer know how to speak Japanese. Is this clear?"

"But—it was because of my knowledge of your language that I was hired by Yumimoto!"

"That doesn't matter. I am ordering you not to understand Japanese anymore."

"That's impossible. No one could obey an order like that."

"There is always a means of obeying. That's what Western brains need to understand."

Now, we're getting to it, I thought.

"Perhaps the Japanese brain is capable of forcing itself to forget a language. The Western brain doesn't have that facility."

This absurd argument seemed admissible to Mister Saito.

"Try all the same. Pretend. I have been given orders. Do you understand?"

When I returned to my desk, my face must have been wearing a strange expression because Fubuki looked at me with tender concern. I sat quietly for a long time, wondering what I should do.

Quitting would have been the most logical thing. And yet I could not quite resign myself to this idea. To Western eyes, there would have been nothing ignominious in this; to Japanese eyes, it meant losing face. I had been at Yumimoto barely a month, but I had signed a year's contract. Leaving after so short a time would have brought disgrace on me—in their eyes as well as in my own.

Besides, I had absolutely no desire to leave. I had gone to some trouble to get a job at this company: I had studied Tokyo's business terminology, I had taken language tests. Granted, becoming a leading light in international commerce was never my life's ambition, but I had always had a yearning to live in the country I had worshiped since early childhood.

I would stay.

I therefore had to find a way of obeying Mister Saito's order. I probed my brain in search of a layer favorable to amnesia. Were there any *oubliette* cells in my neuronal fortress? Alas, the edifice had its strengths and weaknesses, its watchtowers and sculleries, but nothing that would accommodate permanently entombing a language I heard spoken around me all the time.

Could I pretend to forget? If languages were a forest, would I be able to hide behind the French beeches, the English limes, the Latin oaks, the Greek olive trees—and of course the towering Japanese Cryptomeria cedars (whose name now seemed perfectly suited)?

Mori, Fubuki's patronym, meant "forest." Perhaps that was why, at that very moment, I was looking at her helplessly. I realized that she was still watching me, an inquisitive look in her eye.

She stood up and beckoned me to follow her to the kitchen. I slumped into a chair.

"What did he say to you?" she asked.

I poured my heart out. My voice was convulsed with emotion, I was on the brink of tears. I could no longer hold back what was building up inside me.

"I hate Mister Saito! He's a bastard and an idiot."

Fubuki smiled slightly.

"No. You're wrong."

"*You* can say that because you are kind. You don't see any harm. But, I mean, giving me an order like that, he'd have to be some kind of..."

"Calm down. The order didn't come from him. He was passing along instructions from Mister Omochi. He had no choice."

"In that case, it's Mister Omochi who's a..."

She interrupted me.

"He's an exceptional person. He's also the vice-president. There's nothing we can do about it."

"What if I spoke to the president about it. Mister Haneda. What kind of man is he?"

"Mister Haneda is a remarkable man. He is very intelligent and a very good man. Unfortunately, there is no question of your going to him and complaining."

I knew she was right. It would have been inconceivable to skip even one rung in the corporate ladder—let alone several. I only had the right to speak to my immediate superior, who happened to be Miss Mori.

"You're my only hope, Fubuki. I know that there isn't much that you can do for me. But thank you. Your kindness alone does me so much good."

She smiled.

I asked her what the ideogram of her first name was. She showed me her business card. I looked at the *kanji*.

"A snowstorm!" I exclaimed. " 'Fubuki' means 'snowstorm'! I can't believe anyone's actually called that."

"I was born during a snowstorm. My parents saw it as an omen."

The Yumimoto list came to mind: "Mori Fubuki, born in Nara on January 18, 1961. . . ." She was a winter baby. I suddenly imagined the snowstorm over the beautiful town of Nara and its innumerable bells. It made sense that this resplendent young woman should have been born on a day when the pristine, crystalline wonders of the sky drifted down upon one of the most beautiful landscapes on earth.

She told me about her childhood in Kansai. I told her about mine, in the same province, in a village called Shukugawa, not far from Nara and near Mount Kabuto.

Invoking these mythological places brought tears to my eyes.

"I'm so glad we're both daughters of Kansai! That's where the heart of the old Japan still beats."

I was five years old when we left the Japanese mountains for the Chinese desert. That first exile made such a deep impression on me that I had felt I would do anything to return to the country that for so long I thought of as my native land.

When we returned to our desks, I still had no solution to my amnesia problem. I knew less than ever about my status within the Yumimoto Corporation. But I had a great feeling of inner peace. I was a colleague of Fubuki Mori.

I DID WHAT I could to give the impression of being busy while also appearing not to understand a word of what was being said around me. I served the managers cups of tea and coffee without a whisper of a polite reply, or responding to their thanks. They were unaware of the orders I was under, and therefore mildly astonished that the friendly white geisha had transformed herself into a Yankee with no manners and nothing to say for herself.

Unfortunately, the *ôchakumi* didn't take up much time. I

decided, without asking anyone's permission, to distribute the mail.

This meant pushing an enormous metal trolley and passing by each desk. The work suited me. It allowed me to make use of my linguistic competence, since most of the addresses were in ideograms—and because I was beyond Mister Saito's sphere of influence I didn't need to hide the fact that I understood Japanese. I quickly discovered that memorizing the employee list hadn't been a waste of time. Not only could I identify every single employee, I could also use the opportunity, if it arose, to wish them—or their wife or progeny—a happy birthday.

"Here's your mail, Mister Shiranai," I would say with a smile and a bow, "and a happy birthday to your little Yoshiro, three today!"

This always earned me a disbelieving stare.

Distributing the mail took me all the longer because I had to travel throughout the entire Import-Export Division, which spread out over two gigantic floors. Accompanied by my trolley, which gave me a pleasingly industrious appearance, I spent endless amounts of time on the elevator—down to the mailroom, up to the forty-third floor, down to the mailroom, up to the forty-fourth floor. I liked this because just next to where I stood and waited for the elevator was the huge bay window. That was when I would indulge in what I called "throwing myself into the view." I glued my nose to the window and imagined myself falling. The city was so far below that before I hurtled into the ground, I could look leisurely and appreciatively at everything around me.

I had found my vocation. This simple, useful, human task was so conducive to contemplation that I decided I wouldn't have minded doing it for the rest of my life.

MISTER SAITO SUMMONED me to his office. I was treated to a well-deserved telling-off. I had committed the crime of showing initiative. I had taken a function upon myself without asking for permission from my direct superiors. What's more, the Import-Export Division's actual mail delivery boy, who came in the afternoons, was on the brink of a nervous breakdown because he thought he was about to be laid off.

"Stealing someone else's job is a very serious offense," Mister Saito told me, quite rightly.

I was devastated that my promising career had ended so soon. Apart from anything else, the problem of what I should do with myself presented itself again.

I had an idea, one that in my innocence appeared luminously clever. In the course of my wandering around the company I had noticed that every office had one or several wall calendars that were hardly ever up-to-date, either because the adjustable red frame had not been moved forward to the correct date, or because the page for a new month had not been turned over.

This time I did not forget to ask for permission.

"Mister Saito, could I put the calendars to the correct date?"

He answered yes without really thinking about it.

Every morning I went into each office and moved the little red frame to the appropriate date. I had a position: I was the calendar-turner.

Little by little, employees realized what I was doing. It spawned hilarity.

"Are you doing okay?" they would ask. "This undertaking isn't exhausting you too much?"

"Oh, it's terrible," I would answer with a smile. "But I'm taking vitamins."

My new job had the inconvenience of not taking up enough time, but it did allow me to use the elevator, and therefore to throw myself into the view. It had the added benefit of entertaining my colleagues.

A sort of professional pinnacle arrived when we went from February to March. It was not enough simply to adjust the red frame on that day. I had to turn over an entire page, sometimes even tear off the February page.

The employees greeted me as you would a champion athlete. I assassinated the months of February with sweeping gestures, like a samurai, miming a merciless struggle against—in this case—a giant photograph of a snow-covered Mount Fuji. Then I would leave the battlefield, feigning exhaustion, with the sober pride of a victorious warrior, to the *banzais!* of my delighted spectators.

Word of my glory reached the ears of Mister Saito. I expected a towering telling-off for having played the fool and had therefore prepared my defense.

"You gave me permission to make the calendars up-to-date," I began before even being subjected to his fury.

He replied not with anger but with his usual tone of simple displeasure.

"Yes. You may continue. But stop making a spectacle of yourself. You're distracting the employees."

I was amazed by so light a reprimand.

"Photocopy this for me," he added.

He handed me a huge sheaf of pages. There must have been a thousand of them.

I put the sheaf into the automatic feed of the photocopier, which executed the task with exemplary speed and courtesy. I delivered the original and the copies to my superior.

He called me back.

"Your photocopies are slightly crooked," he said, holding up one sheet. "Start over."

I went back to the photocopier, thinking I must have put the pages into the automatic feed at a slight angle. This time I gave the task my utmost attention. The results looked impeccable. I took my *oeuvre* back to Mister Saito.

"They're crooked again," he told me.

"That's not true!" I cried.

"It's extremely bad manners to say that to your superior."

"I'm sorry. But I made sure that the photocopying was perfect."

"It isn't. Look."

He showed me one page, which I thought irreproachably straight.

"What's wrong with it?"

"The text is not absolutely parallel to the edge of the page."

"Do you think so?"

"If I say so, yes!"

He threw the sheaf of paper into his wastepaper basket.

"Are you using the automatic feed?"

"Indeed I am."

"That explains it. Don't use the automatic feed. It's not accurate enough."

"Mister Saito, if I don't use the automatic feed it'll take me hours to get to through all this."

"Where's the problem?" He smiled. "You didn't have enough to do as it was."

I understood: this was my punishment for the business with the calendars.

I installed myself at the photocopier as if it were the galley of a ship. Each time I had to lift up the top, place the page face-down with minute precision, press the button, and check the results. It was three o'clock when I started on my treadmill. At seven o'clock I still had not finished. Employees came by from time to time. If they had more than ten copies to do, I would humbly ask them to consent to use the machine at the other end of the corridor.

I glanced at the contents of what I was photocopying. They were the rules of the golf club of which Mister Saito was a member. I started to laugh.

The next minute I felt more like crying, thinking about all the innocent trees that my superior was wasting to chastise me. I imagined the forests of the Japan of my childhood—maples, cedars, and ginkgoes—felled for the sole purpose of punishing a creature as insignificant as myself. I remembered, again, that Fubuki's family name meant "forest."

Then along came Mister Tenshi, director of the Dairy Products Department. He held the same position as Mister Saito, who was manager of the General Accounting Department. I looked at him in amazement. Surely someone in his position delegated his photocopying.

He answered my unspoken question.

"It's eight o'clock. I'm the only person in my office. Tell me, why don't you use the automatic feed?"

I told him with a humble smile that I was following specific instructions from Mister Saito.

"I see," he said in a voice full of hidden meaning.

He seemed lost in thought for a while, then spoke.

"You're from Belgium, aren't you?"

"Yes."

"What a happy coincidence. I've got a very interesting project involving your country. Could you find the time to do a report for me?"

I gazed at him as one might the Messiah. He explained that a Belgian cooperative had developed a new process for removing the fat content of butter.

"I believe in low-fat butter," he said. "It's the future."

"I've always thought so, too," I replied, inventing an opinion on the spot.

"Come and see me in my office tomorrow."

I finished my photocopying in a trance. A career opportunity was opening up before me. I put the sheaf of paper on Mister Saito's table and left, triumphant.

WHEN I ARRIVED at work the next day, Fubuki looked at me with a frightened expression.

"Mister Saito wants you to start the photocopying again. He thinks the pages are crooked."

I burst out laughing and told her about the little game in which our boss seemed to be indulging himself on my account.

"I'm sure that he hasn't even looked at the latest photocopies. I did them one by one, calibrated to the nearest millimeter. I don't know how many hours I spent on it— all this for his golf club's rules and regulations."

"He's torturing you!"

I reassured her.

"Don't worry. He's keeping me amused."

I went back to the photocopier, which I was beginning to know very well, and entrusted the work to the automatic feed. I was convinced that Mister Saito would announce his verdict without paying the least attention to my work. I felt a wave of emotion when I thought of Fubuki. She was so kind. Thank goodness she was there.

In the end, Mister Saito's predictable reaction suited me perfectly. The day before, I had spent more than seven hours producing the thousand photocopies one by one. That gave me an excellent alibi for the hours that I would spend in Mister Tenshi's office. The automatic feed did the job in about ten minutes. I picked up my tome and slipped away to the Dairy Products Department.

Mister Tenshi gave me contact numbers for the Belgian cooperative.

"I will need a full report, with as much detail as possible, on this new low-fat butter. You can sit at Mister Saitama's desk. He's away on business."

"Tenshi" means "angel." I thought he wore his name extremely well. Not only was he giving me a chance, he was leaving me carte blanche, which is exceptional in Japan. And he had taken this initiative without asking for anyone else's opinion.

I was aware this meant he was running a considerable risk. I consequently felt an instant, boundless devotion to Mister Tenshi—the devotion that every Japanese worker owes to his boss, the devotion I had been unable to feel toward Mister Saito or Mister Omochi. Mister Tenshi had suddenly become my commander, my captain-in-arms. Like a samurai, I was prepared to fight to the death for him.

I threw myself into the battle of low-fat butter. The time difference meant that I could not call Belgium immediately, so I started by talking to Japanese consumer organizations and to people at the Department of Health, to learn what the dietary habits of the Japanese population were with respect to butter, and what effects they were having on average cholesterol levels. The average Japanese citizen, I discovered, was eating more and more butter. Obesity and cardiovascular diseases were gaining ground rapidly.

When the time of day permitted, I called the Belgian cooperative. The thick rural accent in my native tongue on the other end of the line moved me. My compatriot, flattered to be talking on the phone with someone in Japan, was extremely helpful. Ten minutes later, I received a ten-page fax, detailing the new process for removing the fat content of butter for which the cooperative held the patent.

I was compiling the report of the century. It opened with an overview of the Japanese butter market, its growth since 1950, and the parallel growth of health problems linked to excessive consumption of saturated fat. Next I outlined the current processes for removing fat from butter, the new Belgian technique, its considerable advantages, etc. As I had to write this in English, I took the work home with me. I needed my dictionary for the scientific terms. I stayed up all night.

I arrived at Yumimoto two hours early the following morning to type up the report and hand it to Mister Tenshi, so that I wouldn't arrive late at Mister Saito's office.

The latter called me in straightaway.

"I have inspected the photocopying that you left on my desk last night. You're improving, but it is not yet perfect. Start over."

And he threw the pile of paper into the trash.

I bowed my head and complied. I forced myself not to laugh.

Mister Tenshi joined me at the photocopier. He congratulated me with all the warmth that his respectful reserve would allow.

"Your report is excellent and you drafted it with extraordinary speed. In the meeting, would you like me to indicate who its author is?"

This was a man of rare generosity. He would have been committing a professional error had I asked him to.

"Definitely not, Mister Tenshi. That would do you as much harm as it would me."

"You're right. Even so, I could suggest to Mister Saito

and Mister Omochi in a forthcoming meeting that you would be useful to me. Do you think Mister Saito would take offense?"

"Quite the opposite. Look at the piles of unnecessary photocopying that he has me doing just to get me out of his office. It's obvious he's looking for ways of getting rid of me. He'd be delighted if you offered him an opportunity."

"Then you won't be offended if I attribute your report to myself?"

I was astonished. It was simply not done to show such consideration to an underling.

"Oh, Mister Tenshi, I would be honored if you took credit for it."

We parted in a state of mutual high esteem. I looked forward to the future with confidence. Soon I would be done with Mister Saito's harassment, with the photocopier, and with the absurd ban on speaking my second language.

EVERYTHING ERUPTED SEVERAL days later. I was summoned to Mister Omochi's office. I went into the vice-president's lair without the least apprehension, not knowing why he wanted to see me.

Mister Tenshi was there. He turned toward me and gave

me a smile filled with more humanity than I had ever seen. What it said was, "We're going to endure a terrible ordeal, but we will endure it together."

I thought I knew what it meant to be bawled out. What we underwent there in Mister Omochi's office revealed how ignorant I was. Mister Tenshi and I were subjected to demented screaming. I still wonder which was worse: the content or the delivery.

The content was incredibly insulting. My companion in misfortune and I were called traitors, incompetents, snakes, deceitful, and—the height of injury—individualists.

The delivery explained much about Japanese history. I would have been capable of anything to stop the hideous screaming—invade Manchuria, persecute millions of Chinese, commit suicide for the Emperor, hurl my airplane into an American battleship, perhaps even work for two Yumimoto Corporations.

The most unbearable part was seeing my benefactor humiliated because of me. Mister Tenshi was an intelligent and conscientious man; he had taken a considerable risk for me, and with full knowledge of the facts. He had acted out of pure altruism. As a reward for his kindness, he was being dragged through the mud.

His head was lowered and his shoulders hunched. I tried to follow his example. His face expressed submission and shame. I imitated him. Then the Obese One offered up his most outrageous accusation.

"You've never had any other goal than sabotaging the company!"

Thoughts whirred around inside my head. I could not permit this incident to ruin my guardian angel's chances for advancement. I threw myself into the raging torrent of Mister Omochi's invective.

"Mister Tenshi didn't want to sabotage the company. I begged him to let me work on the report. I alone am responsible."

I just had time to see my companion in misfortune turn to me with a look of alarm. "Don't say anything, for pity's sake!" his eyes were pleading. Alas, too late.

Mister Omochi stood open-mouthed for a moment before coming up to me and bellowing right into my face.

"Do you dare to defend yourself?"

"No, I'm blaming myself. I'm claiming all the wrong for myself. I alone should be punished."

"You dare to defend this snake!"

"Mister Tenshi does not need to be defended. Your accusations against him are misplaced."

I saw my benefactor close his eyes and realized that I had uttered something irreparable.

"You dare to imply that something I say is false? Your bad manners are beyond belief!"

"I wouldn't dare to imply such a thing. I just think that Mister Tenshi has misled you in the hope of absolving me."

With an expression that said that—in our present position—there was nothing further to fear, Mister Tenshi spoke next, all the mortification in the world in his voice.

"I beg you, don't hold it against her. She doesn't know what she's saying. She is a Westerner, she's young, and she has no experience. I have made an indefensible mistake. I am terribly ashamed."

"So you should be! There's no excuse for *you!*" yelled the Obese One.

"However much wrong I have done, I must all the same emphasize the excellence of Amélie-san's report, and the remarkable speed with which she compiled it."

"That is not the point! Mister Saitama should have done this work!"

"He was away on business."

"You should have waited for him to get back."

"This new fat-reduced butter must be the envy of other companies. By the time Mister Saitama had returned from his trip and compiled his report we could have been beaten to it."

"Would you by any chance be calling into question the quality of Mister Saitama's work?"

"Absolutely not. But Mister Saitama doesn't speak French and doesn't know Belgium. He would have found it far more difficult than Amélie-san."

"Be quiet. That disgusting sort of pragmatism is worthy of a Westerner."

I found the Obese One's saying this right in front of me too much to take.

"Forgive my Western indignity. We did something wrong, yes. That doesn't mean there isn't some gain to be made from our mistake...."

Mister Omochi approached me. The expression in his eyes was so terrifying that it stopped me in midsentence.

"I'm warning you. This was your first and last report. Get out! I don't want to see you anymore!"

I didn't wait to be told a second time. In the corridor, I could still hear screams from the mountain of flesh and contrite silence from his victim. Then the door opened and Mister Tenshi joined me. We went to the kitchen together in silence, stunned by the insults that had been heaped on us.

"I'm so sorry for dragging you into this," he said eventually.

"Please, Mister Tenshi, don't apologize. I will be grateful

to you my whole life. You're the only person here who's given me a chance. It was courageous and generous of you. I knew that at the beginning, and I know it even more clearly now that I've seen what it has brought upon you. You shouldn't have told them that I wrote the report."

He stared at me.

"I didn't. Don't you remember our conversation? I wanted to talk about this discreetly at the very top, to Mister Haneda. That was my only hope of achieving anything. By telling Mister Omochi we were only heading for disaster."

"So it was Mister Saito who told the vice-president? What a bastard. He could have made me very happy by getting rid of me—but no, he had to go and . . ."

"Keep what you think about Mister Saito to yourself. It's better that way. And in any case, he wasn't the one who denounced us. I saw the note on Mister Omochi's desk, and I saw who wrote it."

"Mister Saitama?"

"No. Do I really have to tell you?"

"You do."

He sighed.

"The note was signed by Miss Mori."

I felt as if I'd been hit with a club.

"Fubuki? It can't have been."

Mr. Tenshi remained silent.

"I don't believe it!" I cried. "That coward Mister Saito must have told her to write the note. He isn't even brave enough to do his denouncing for himself, so he delegates someone else to do it!"

"You're wrong about Mister Saito. He might be fussy and a bit obtuse, but he's not cruel. He would never have condemned us to the vice-president's anger."

"Fubuki couldn't do a thing like that!"

Mister Tenshi restricted himself to sighing again.

"Why would she do a thing like that?" I went on. "Does she hate you?"

"Oh no. She didn't do it to spite me. When all is said and done, this whole business does *you* more harm than me. I haven't lost anything. But you have missed out on any chance of promotion for a very long time."

"I don't understand. She's always been so friendly toward me."

"Yes, so long as your work consisted of updating calendars and photocopying golf club bylaws."

"But there was no danger of my taking her place!"

"She was never afraid of that."

"Then why denounce me? Why would it upset her if I went to work for you?"

"Miss Mori struggled for years to get the job she has

now. She probably found it unbearable for you to get that sort of promotion after being with the company only ten weeks."

"I can't believe it. That's just so ... mean."

"All I can say is that she suffered greatly during the first few years she was here."

"So she wants me to suffer the same fate? It's too pathetic. I must talk to her."

"Do you really think that's a good idea?"

"Of course. How else are we going to work things out if we don't talk?"

"You just talked to Mister Omochi. Does it strike you that things have been worked out?"

"There's one thing I'm sure of, and that's if you *don't* talk there's no chance of working out the problem."

"And there's one thing I'm even more sure of, and that's if you *do* talk, there's a serious chance you'll make things worse."

"I won't get you involved in this. But I must speak to Fubuki. Otherwise I'll never forgive myself."

MISS MORI ACCEPTED my proposal to talk privately with an expression of astonished curiosity. She

35

followed me to the conference room, which was empty.
We sat down.

I started quietly and soberly.

"I thought we were friends. I don't understand."

"What don't you understand?"

"Are you going to deny that you denounced me."

"I haven't denied anything. I followed the rules."

"Are the rules more important to you than friendship?"

" 'Friendship' is a strong word. I'd prefer 'good relationship between colleagues.' "

She proffered this expression with ingenuous, affable calm.

"I see. Do you think our relationship will continue to be good, after what you've done?"

"If you apologize, I won't bear you a grudge."

"You've got a good sense of humor, Fubuki."

"You're behaving as if you're the injured party, when you've actually done something very wrong."

I made the mistake of coming out with a sharp retort.

"And I had been thinking that the Japanese were different from the Chinese."

She looked at me, not understanding. I went on.

"Yes. The Chinese didn't have to wait for Communism to consider denunciation a virtue. To this day the Chinese in Singapore, for example, still encourage their children to

36

tell on their little friends. I thought the Japanese had a stronger sense of honor."

I had definitely upset her. A strategic mistake.

She smiled.

"Do you think you're in a position to teach me anything about morals?"

"Why do you think I wanted to talk to you, Fubuki?"

"Because you weren't thinking."

"Hasn't it occurred to you that I might want a reconciliation?"

"Fine. You apologize and we'll be reconciled."

I sighed.

"You're quick and intelligent. Why are you pretending you don't understand?"

"Don't try and get above yourself. You're very easy to figure out."

"Good. Then you can see why I'm so indignant."

"I can see why and I disapprove of your reasons. I'm the one who had some reason to feel indignant about your attitude. You had your eye on a promotion to which you had no right."

"Fine. I had no right to it. But what harm could it actually do you? My opportunity didn't cheat you out of anything."

"I'm twenty-nine years old. You're twenty-two. I've been

in this position since last year. I fought for it for years. Did you think that you were going to get a comparable job within a matter of weeks?"

"So that's it. You want to see me suffer. You can't bear other people's opportunities. How childish."

She gave a scornful little laugh.

"And do you think that making your situation worse is proof of maturity? I'm your superior. Do you think you have the right to be so rude to me?"

"You're right. You're my superior. I have no right, I know. But I wanted you to know how disappointed I am. I really thought highly of you."

She laughed elegantly.

"I'm not disappointed. I didn't think highly of you."

WHEN I ARRIVED at work the following morning, Miss Mori informed me of my new appointment.

"You won't be changing departments. You'll be working here, in accounting."

I felt like laughing.

"Me, in accounting? Why not ask me to be a trapeze artist?"

" 'Accounting' may be overstating things. I don't think

38

you are capable of bookkeeping," she said with a pitying smile.

She showed me a large drawer in which the invoices for the last few weeks had been piled up. Then she showed me the shelves with rows of enormous ledgers, each bearing the initials of one of Yumimoto's eleven import-export departments.

"Your assignment couldn't be more simple, and therefore well within your abilities. First, you have to arrange the invoices in chronological order. Then, you work out which department each one belongs to. Take this one, for example: eleven million for Finnish Emmental. How very funny—it involves the Dairy Products Department. You take the ledger marked 'DP' and copy out into each of the columns the date, the name of the company, and the sum. When you've sorted and recorded all the invoices, you file them in this drawer here."

There was no denying the fact that this was not difficult work.

"Isn't everything computerized?"

"Yes. At the end of the month, Mister Unaji will input all of the invoices into the computer. All he will have to do is to copy out your work. It will hardly take him any time at all."

For the first two days I sometimes had trouble figuring out which invoice went where. When I asked Fubuki, she replied with irritated courtesy.

"What's Reming Ltd?"

"Nonferrous metals. Department MM."

"What's Gunzer GMBH?"

"Chemicals. Department CP."

I very quickly got to know all the companies and the departments to which they belonged. My assignment seemed to get easier and easier. It was exquisitely boring, which did not displease me, for it allowed me to put my mind elsewhere. While I sorted through the invoices, I would often look up and daydream as I admired the ravishing face of my denouncer.

Weeks went by. I fell more and more into a state of contentment I called "invoice serenity." There was very little difference between what I was doing and a monk transcribing illuminated manuscripts in the Middle Ages. I spent entire days copying out letters and numbers. Never in my life had so little been asked of my brain, and it experienced extraordinary tranquillity—a sort of Zen of accounting. I was surprised to find myself thinking that if I spent forty years immersed in such voluptuous mindlessness, I would not complain.

To think that I had been silly enough to get a college degree. There can be nothing less intellectually stimulating than repetition. I was devoted to order, not thought, I now realized. Writing down numbers while contemplating beauty was happiness itself.

Fubuki had been right, after all. I had chosen the wrong path with Mister Tenshi. I had compiled that report for the wrong reasons, you could say. My mind was not that of a conqueror, but that of a cow that spends its life chewing contentedly in the meadow of invoices, waiting for the train of eternal grace to pass by. How good it felt to exist without pride or ambition. To live in hibernation.

AT THE END of the month Mister Unaji input my work onto the computer. It took him two days to copy out my rows of numbers and letters. I felt ridiculously proud to have been a link in the efficient chain.

Chance—or was it fate?—dictated that he kept the accounts for the "CP" ledger for last. As he had with the first ten account books, he started tapping on his keyboard without batting an eyelid. A few minutes later I heard him exclaiming, "I don't believe it! I don't believe it!"

He turned the pages with increasing frenzy. Then he

succumbed to a burst of nervous laughter that gradually mutated into a succession of halting little cries. The forty members of the office watched him in stupefied silence.

I started to feel very uncomfortable.

Fubuki got up and ran over to him. He showed her some passages from the ledger and roared with laughter. She turned toward me. She did not share in her colleague's unhealthy hilarity. Ashen, she called me over.

"What's this?" she asked tartly, pointing out one of the incriminating lines.

I read the line.

"Well, it's an invoice from GmbH, dated the . . ."

"GMBH? GMBH?" she said furiously.

The entire Accounting Department burst out laughing. I didn't understand.

"Can you explain to me what 'GmbH' is?" my superior asked, folding her arms.

"It's a German chemical company we deal with very frequently."

The roars of laughter redoubled.

"Didn't you notice that 'GmbH' was always preceded by one or several names?" continued Fubuki.

"Yes. I assumed they were the names of its various subsidiaries. I thought it was better not to clog up the ledger with the details."

Even the inhibited Mister Saito gave free rein to his mounting amusement. Fubuki was still not laughing. Her face displayed the most terrifyingly restrained rage. If she could have slapped me, she would have. Her voice sliced the air like a saber.

"Idiot! 'GmbH' is the German equivalent of the American 'Inc.', the English 'Ltd.', or the French 'S.A.' The companies that you have so brilliantly amalgamated under 'GmbH' haven't got anything to do with each other! It's as if you decided to write 'Ltd.' for every English and Canadian company we deal with! How long is it going to take you to correct these mistakes?"

I chose the stupidest defense possible.

"Trust the Germans to come up with such a long-winded way of saying 'Inc.'!"

"That's right! It must be the Germans' fault you're so stupid!"

"Calm down, Fubuki. How could I know..."

"How could you *not* know! Your country has a border with Germany and you still didn't know, whereas we, who live on the other side of the planet, know full well!"

I was about to say something that, thank heavens, I kept to myself: "Belgium may well have a border with Germany, but during the last war, Japan had far more in common with Germany than a border!"

43

I contented myself with bowing my head, defeated.

"Don't stand there like a statue! Go and find all the invoices you have so brilliantly filed under 'chemicals' for the last month!"

I opened the drawer and almost felt like laughing when I realized that as a result of my filing technique the files for "chemical companies" had reached astonishing proportions.

Mister Unaji, Miss Mori, and I set to work. It took us three days to sort out the eleven different creditors. I was already in the doghouse with them when an even more serious calamity erupted.

The first sign was a sort of trembling in the good Mister Unaji's large shoulders. It meant that he was starting to laugh. The vibrations spread to his chest and then to his throat. Eventually came the laugh. I broke out in goose pimples.

Fubuki was already white with fury.

"What's she done *now*?"

With one hand Mister Unaji showed her the original invoice and with the other the accounts book.

She hid her face in her hands. I felt sick.

Then they turned several pages and pointed to various invoices. In the end, Fubuki grabbed hold of my arm.

Without a word, she showed me the figures copied out in my inimitable writing.

"Whenever there are more than four zeros in a row, you didn't bother to copy them out! You took away or added at least one zero each time!"

"Oh yes, so I did."

"Do you have any idea what this means? How many weeks it will take to find all your mistakes and correct them?"

"It's not easy—all those enormously long lines of zeros . . ."

"Be quiet!"

Pulling me by the arm, she led me outside. We went into an empty office and she shut the door.

"Aren't you ashamed of yourself?"

"I'm terribly sorry," I replied pathetically.

"No, you're not! Do you think I can't see what you're doing? You made these incomprehensible mistakes to get your revenge on me!"

"I swear I didn't."

"I know you did. You resent me so much for telling the vice-president about the business with the Dairy Products Department that you've decided to make a fool of me in public."

"It's me that I'm making a fool of, not you."

"I'm your direct superior and everyone knows I gave you this job. I am therefore responsible for what you do. And you know that. Your despicable behavior is typical of Westerners. You put your personal vanity ahead of the interests of the company. You didn't hesitate before sabotaging Yumimoto's accounts to get your revenge on me, knowing perfectly well that your mistakes would fall on my shoulders!"

"I had no idea, and I didn't make these mistakes on purpose."

"Oh come on! I know that you're not very intelligent, but nobody could be stupid enough to make mistakes like that!"

"Yes they could: me."

"Stop it! I know you're lying."

"Fubuki, I give you my word of honor that I did not copy them out incorrectly on purpose."

"Honor! What would you know about honor?"

She laughed scornfully.

"Believe it or not, honor does exist in the West too."

"Ah! And you find it honorable to admit openly that you are the stupidest person on earth?"

"I don't think I'm all *that* stupid."

"You're either a traitor or you're a half-wit. There's no third option."

"There *are* normal people who are incapable of copying out rows of numbers."

"That sort of person doesn't exist in Japan."

"Who would dream of challenging Japanese superiority?" I was actually trying to sound contrite.

"You should have told me you were mentally handicapped, instead of letting me entrust you with this work."

"I didn't know. I'd never copied out rows of numbers in my life."

"It's a peculiar kind of handicap. It doesn't take a scrap of intelligence to transcribe figures."

"I think that's precisely the problem with people like me. If our intelligence isn't required, our brains go to sleep. Hence my mistakes."

Fubuki's face at last lost its combative expression. She assumed an air of bemusement.

"Your intelligence has to be required? What a quaint idea."

"It couldn't be more normal."

"Fine. I'll think of some work that will require intelligence," my superior repeated, apparently delighting in this turn of phrase.

"In the meantime, shall I go and help Mister Unaji correct my mistakes?"

"Certainly not! You've done enough damage as it is!"

I DON'T KNOW how long it took my unfortunate colleague to restore order to the ledgers I had so systematically disfigured. But it took two days for Miss Mori to find an assignment she deemed within my capabilities.

A massive file was waiting for me on my desk when I arrived in the morning.

"You will doublecheck all the expenses for business trips," she informed me.

"More accounting? But I *have* warned you about my deficiencies."

"That won't matter this time. This work will require your intelligence," she explained with a sardonic smile.

She opened the file.

"Here, for example, is the file that Mister Shiranai has put together so that he can be reimbursed for his expenses for his trip to Düsseldorf. You will have to go over every sum and see if you get the same total to the nearest yen. As most of the bills are in German marks, you will have to work out the sums based on the rates of exchange on the dates indicated on each bill. Don't forget that the rate changes every day."

So began one of the worst nightmares of my life. From the moment I was given this new task, time disappeared into an eternal tunnel of torture. Never, but never, did I manage to reach a total that was even remotely close to those I was supposed to be double-checking. For example, if an employee had calculated that Yumimoto owed him 93,327 yen, I would get 15,211 yen, or perhaps 172,045. It was very soon clear that the errors fell in my camp.

At the end of the first day I approached Fubuki.

"I don't think I'm capable of carrying out this assignment."

"And yet this is work that requires intelligence," she replied, implacable.

"I can't work it out," I admitted miserably.

"You'll get used to it."

I didn't get used to it. I was, to the last possible degree and despite determined efforts on my part, incapable.

My superior decided to demonstrate how easy it was. She opened one of the files and started to work. Her fingers flew with lightning speed across her calculator. She didn't even have to look at the keypad. I timed her. She was done in less than four minutes.

"I get the same figure as Mister Saitama, to the nearest yen."

She put her stamp on the report.

Subjugated by this latest injustice of nature, I returned to my labors. Twelve hours were not enough for me to do what had taken Fubuki a trifling three minutes and fifty seconds.

I don't know how many days passed before she realized that I had not yet finished double-checking a single file.

"Not even one!" she exclaimed.

"No, not even one," I admitted, expecting the worst.

To my dismay, she was content simply to point to the calendar.

"Don't forget that all the files need to be finished by the end of the month."

I would have preferred she start screaming.

More days passed. I was in hell, assailed by streams of numbers and commas and decimal points that coagulated in my brain into an opaque magma, so that I could no longer distinguish them from each other. An optometrist assured me my eyesight was fine.

Figures, whose calm Pythagorean beauty I had always admired, became my enemies. The calculator, too, was set against me. Among my many psychomotor problems was one that was particularly debilitating. When I had to tap on a keypad for more than five minutes at a time, my hand suddenly became as sluggish as if I had sunk it into a sticky pile of mashed potatoes. Four of my fingers became irremediably immobilized; only the index finger managed to reach the keys, but did so incomprehensibly slowly and awkwardly.

Given that this phenomenon was coupled with my singular stupidity on the subject of numbers, I presented a fairly disconcerting spectacle. I started looking at each new number with as much astonishment as Robinson Crusoe spying a footprint in the sand. My numbed hand tried to reproduce it on the keyboard. To achieve this, my head kept having to make trips back and forth between the paper and the screen, to ensure that I hadn't misplaced a comma or a zero someplace along the way. Strangely, this painstaking process still didn't prevent me from committing even more colossal errors.

One day as I was tapping away pitifully, I looked up and saw my superior observing me with consternation.

"What *is* your problem?" she asked.

I told her about the mashed-potato syndrome paralyzing my hand. I thought it might make her feel more sympathetic. But her facial expression was eloquent. And what it said was, "I understand now: she really is mentally handicapped. This explains everything."

THE END OF the month was drawing near and the pile of reimbursement files was as thick as ever.

"Are you sure you're not doing it on purpose?"

"Absolutely sure."

"Are there many...people like you in your country?"

I was the first Belgian she had met. I felt a rush of national pride.

"There are no other Belgians like me."

"That's reassuring."

I burst out laughing.

"You find this amusing?"

"Has anyone ever told you, Fubuki, that it is wrong to mistreat the mentally impaired?"

"Yes. But I wasn't warned that I would ever have one working for me."

I laughed harder.

"I still don't see what you find so amusing."

"It must be part of my psychomotor illness."

"You'd do better to concentrate on your work."

THREE DAYS BEFORE the end of the month, I announced my decision not to go home in the evenings.

"With your permission, I will spend the night here at my desk."

"Is your brain more efficient in the dark?" Fubuki asked.

"Let's hope so. Perhaps being alone will help."

I got her permission without difficulty. It was not unusual for employees to stay at the office all night when deadlines were looming.

"Do you think one night will be enough?"

"Probably not. I don't intend to go home before the end of the month."

I showed her my backpack.

"I've brought what I need."

I WAS OVERWHELMED by a feeling of intoxication when I found myself alone in the Accounting Department. It dissipated as soon as I established that my brain worked no better at night than it did during the day. I worked nonstop. This produced absolutely no results.

At four in the morning I went and splashed water on my face, then changed clothes, drank a strong cup of tea, and returned to my desk.

The first employees arrived at seven o'clock. Fubuki arrived an hour later. She glanced at the pigeonhole where the completed expense forms would have been placed and saw that it was still empty. She shook her head.

Another sleepless night followed. The situation remained unchanged. My head was no clearer. And yet I was far from despairing; I felt an incomprehensible surge of optimism, which gave me a certain audacity. Without interrupting my calculations, I therefore conducted conversations with my superior on subjects that were far from relevant.

"Your first name has the word 'snow' in it. In the Japanese version of my name there is 'rain.' That strikes me as very pertinent. There is the same difference between you and me as between snow and rain. Which doesn't alter the fact that we are made of exactly the same substance."

"Do you really think you and I have anything in common?"

I laughed. Lack of sleep had made me giddy. I would sometimes feel deeply tired and dispirited, then suddenly start giggling.

My Danaides' jar was constantly filling with figures that my feeble brain managed to empty out again. I was the Sisyphus of accounting, and like the mythical hero I never gave up. I tackled the inexorable operations for the hundredth time, the thousandth time. I should point out, in passing, this astonishing fact: I got everything wrong a thousand times. This would have been as maddening as a repetitive piece of music except that no two mistakes were alike. For each calculation I got a thousand different results. I was brilliant.

I continued from time to time to look up between sums to contemplate she who had sentenced me to this torture. I was still mesmerized by her beauty. Her only flaw was the overly immaculate way she blow-dried her shoulder-length hair, immobilizing it into an imperturbable curve so rigid that it seemed to say, "I am a female executive." I would succumb to the delicious fantasy of changing her hairstyle. I would set her dazzlingly black hair free. I teased it mentally to make it seem carefree. Sometimes I really let myself go and made her hair look like she had just spent a night of torrid love. She was quite sublime when she looked wild and abandoned.

Fubuki caught me staring at her hair.

"Why are you looking at me like that?"

"I was thinking that in Japanese 'hair' and 'god' are the same word."

"'Paper,' too, don't forget. Get back to your work."

My mental haze was getting worse by the hour. I knew less and less clearly what I should and should not say.

While I was looking up the rate of exchange for the Swedish Crown on February 20th of the year before, my mouth began to speak on its own initiative.

"What did you want to be when you were little?"

"An archery champion."

"That would have been perfect for you!"

As she didn't return the question, I kept going.

"When I was little I wanted to become God. The Christian God with a capital 'G.' When I was about five I realized this would never happen. So I put a little water in my wine and decided to become Christ. I imagined myself dying on the cross before all of humanity. When I was seven, I realized that this was never going to happen. So I decided to become a martyr, and stuck to this choice for many years. It didn't work either."

"And then?"

"You know what happened then. I got a job in accounting at the Yumimoto Corporation. I can't sink any lower."

"You think not?" she asked with a strange smile.

THE LAST NIGHT of the month had arrived. Fubuki was the last to leave. I wondered why she didn't just tell me to go home. It was obvious I would never be able to complete even a fraction of my work.

I was alone again. My third sleepless night in a row in the gigantic office. I was tapping away on the calculator and noting down the increasingly incongruous results.

Then the most fantastic thing happened: my mind flipped.

Suddenly I was weightless. I got up. I was free. I had never been so free in all my life. I walked over to the bay window and looked down on the glittering city far below me. I ruled the world! I was God! I threw my body out of the window to be rid of it.

I switched off the neon lights. The lights below provided enough illumination to see clearly. I went to the kitchen to get a Coke, which I drank without stopping. When I returned to my desk I untied my shoelaces and threw off shoes. I leapt up onto a desk, then hopped from desk to desk, whooping with joy.

My clothes hampered me, so I took them off one by one, scattering them around me. When I was naked I did a handstand. I'd never been able to do that before in my life. I walked over all the nearby desks on my hands. Then, after executing a perfect flip, I leapt up and found myself sitting in my superior's place.

"Fubuki, I am God. Even if you don't believe in me, I am God. You give the orders, but they don't mean much. I rule. I'm not interested in power. It is so much more perfect to rule. You have no idea of my glory. Glory is a wonderful thing. It means having angels trumpet in my honor. I have never been as glorious as I am tonight. All thanks to you. You don't know it, but you have given rise to my glory!

"Pontius Pilate didn't know either that his deeds hastened Christ's triumph. There was the Christ of the olive grove. I am the Christ of computers. The darkness that surrounds contains a mature forest of computers.

"I am looking at your computer, Fubuki. It is magnificent. In the shadows it looks like one of those statues on Easter Island. It is after midnight, meaning it is Friday, my Good Friday, known as the day of Venus in France and the day of gold in Japan, though I can't find any connection whatsoever between Judaeo-Christian suffering, Latin sensuality, and Japanese adoration of an incorruptible metal.

"Since I left the secular world behind to take up holy orders, time has lost all meaning and been transformed into a calculator onto which I tap out numbers riddled with mistakes. I think that it's Easter. From the heights of this Tower of Babel, I see Ueno Park and the trees are covered in snow. Cherry trees in blossom. Easter.

"I've always found Easter as uplifting as Christmas is depressing. A god that becomes a baby is kind of worrisome. Some poor martyr who becomes God—well, that's another matter."

I put my arms round Fubuki's computer and showered it with kisses.

"I'm a poor crucified creature too. The best thing about crucifixion is that it's the end. My suffering will end. They've crammed my body with numbers so numberless that there's no more room for even a decimal point. They will slice my head off with a saber. I won't feel anything.

"It is a very great thing to know when you are going to die, Fubuki. You can prepare yourself and make your last day into a work of art. In the morning my torturers will arrive and I will tell them: 'I have failed! Kill me. But grant me one last wish: Let Fubuki be my executioner. Let her unscrew my head like the top of a peppermill. My blood will flow and it will be black pepper. Drink ye of it: For this is my pepper of the new testament, which is shed for many for the remission of sins. Sneeze in remembrance of me.'"

Suddenly, I realized how cold it was. I could hug the computer to me as tight as possible but I knew it wouldn't keep me warm. I put my clothes back on. My teeth were still chattering. I lay down on the ground and dumped the contents of Fubuki's wastebasket over myself. I lost consciousness.

SOMEONE WAS STANDING over me shouting. I opened my eyes and saw bits of trash. I closed them again.

I slipped back into the abyss.

I heard Fubuki's gentle voice.

"That's just like her. She's covered herself in garbage so that we won't dare touch her. She's made herself untouchable. That's what she's like. She has no dignity. When I tell her that she's stupid she tells me that it's more serious than that, that she's mentally retarded. She always has to put herself down. She thinks that it makes her less of a target. She's wrong."

I wanted to explain that the trash protected me from the cold. I didn't have the strength to speak. Huddled under Fubuki's garbage, I was warm. I went under again.

I EMERGED. THROUGH a layer of crumpled paper, empty soda cans, and cigarette stubs soaked in Coke, I saw the clock. Ten in the morning.

I stood up. No one dared to look at me, except Fubuki.

"Next time you decide to dress up as a tramp, don't do it on our premises. There are subway stations for that sort of thing."

Sick with shame, I took my backpack and fled to the bathroom, where I changed and washed my hair under the tap. When I came back, someone had already cleaned up the traces of my madness.

"I wanted to clean it up myself," I said.

"Yes," commented Fubuki, "You might at least have been capable of that."

"I imagine you're thinking about the expense reports. You're right. It's beyond my abilities. I can solemnly announce that I renounce the task."

"You took your time," she observed snidely.

So that's what it was, I thought. *She wanted me to say it. Obviously. It's much more humiliating.*

"The deadline is end of day," I continued.

"Give me the files."

Two hours later, she had finished the entire stack.

I SPENT THE day like a zombie. I was hung over. My desk was smothered in wads of crumpled paper covered in erroneous sums. I threw them away one by one.

I found it hard not to giggle when I saw Fubuki work-

61

ing at her computer. I pictured myself the night before, sitting naked on the keyboard, my arms and legs wrapped around the machine. And now there she was, placing her delicate fingers on the keys. It was the first time I'd felt any interest in computing.

The few hours sleep I had had under the trash had not been enough to extricate my brain from the fog of numbers. I was wading through the wastes, looking for the ruins of my mental landmarks. Meanwhile, I was already feeling a relief that was almost miraculous: for the first time in weeks, I was not tapping away at a calculator.

I was rediscovering a numberless world. I was coming back down to earth. It seemed strange that after my night of madness, things continued as if nothing serious had happened. Granted, no one had seen me hopping naked from desk to desk on my hands, or French kissing a computer. But I had after all been found asleep under the contents of a wastebasket. In many other countries I might have been thrown out for that kind of behavior.

There is a singular logic to this. You find the most outrageous deviants in the countries with the most authoritarian systems. These countries also show relative tolerance toward staggeringly bizarre behavior. No one knows what "eccentric" truly means until they've met a Japanese eccentric. I slept under the trash in the offices of a major corporation? So what. Japan is a country that knows the meaning of "losing it."

I started playing my little bit parts again. It would be difficult to describe the pleasure with which I served tea and coffee. These simple gestures, which posed absolutely no challenge to my poor brain, helped me put myself back together.

As discreetly as possible, I started updating the calendars again. I forced myself to look busy the whole time, so afraid was I of being sent back to the numbers.

A great event crept up on me before I knew what had happened. I met God. The loathsome vice-president had asked me for a beer, probably thinking that he wasn't fat enough as it was. I brought it to him with an air of polite disgust. I was just leaving the Obese One's lair when the door to the neighboring office opened. I was face to face with none other than the president himself of the Import-Export Division of the Yumimoto Corporation.

We looked at each other in amazement. My dumbfoundedness was understandable; there I was, face to face with the lord of Yumimoto. His was less easy to explain. Did he even know I existed?

"You must be Amélie-san," he said, in a voice that was extraordinarily beautiful and refined.

He smiled and extended his hand. I was so amazed that I couldn't produce a sound. Mister Haneda was a man of about fifty, with a slim body and an exceptionally elegant face. An aura of profound goodness and harmony emanated from him. He looked at me with such genuine goodwill that I lost what little composure I still had.

He left. I stood alone in the corridor, incapable of moving. The president of this place of torture—in which each and every day I was subjected to humiliations each more absurd than the one before—the master of this Gehenna was this magnificent entity!

It surpassed understanding. A company managed by a man of such manifest nobility should have been a paradise of refinement, a place of fulfillment and gentleness. Could it be possible that God reigned over hell?

I was still frozen in stupor when the answer to my question was delivered unto me. The door to Mister Omochi's office opened.

"What the hell are you doing there? You're not being paid to hang around in the hallways!"

All was explained. At Yumimoto, God was president, and the Devil vice-president.

———

FUBUKI, ON THE other hand, was neither God nor the Devil; she was Japanese.

Not all Japanese women are beautiful. But when one of them sets out to be beautiful, anyone else had better stand back.

All forms of beauty are poignant, Japanese beauty particularly so. That lily-white complexion, those mellow eyes, the inimitable shape of the nose, the well-defined contours of the mouth, and the complicated sweetness of the features are enough, by themselves, to eclipse the most perfectly assembled faces.

Then there is her comportment, so stylized that it transforms her into a moving work of art.

Finally, and most importantly, beauty that has resisted so many physical and mental corsets, so many constraints, crushing denials, absurd restrictions, dogmas, heartbreaks, such sadism and asphyxiation, and such conspiracies of silence and humiliation—that sort of beauty is a miracle of heroic survival.

Not that the Japanese woman is a victim; far from it. Among the women on this planet, she hasn't actually drawn the shortest straw. She has considerable power. I should know.

No, if the Japanese woman is to be admired—and she

is—it is because she doesn't commit suicide. Society conspires against her from her earliest infancy. Her brain is steadily filled with plaster until it sets: "If you're not married by the time you're twenty-five, you'll have good reason to be ashamed"; "if you laugh, you won't look dignified"; "if your face betrays your feelings, you'll look coarse"; "if you mention the existence of a single body-hair, you're repulsive"; "if a boy kisses you on the cheek in public, you're a whore"; "if you enjoy eating, you're a pig"; "if you take pleasure in sleeping, you're no better than a cow"; and so on. These precepts would be merely anecdotal if they weren't taken so much to heart.

These are the messages that these incongruous dogmas bully into the Japanese woman:

"Do not dare hope for anything beautiful. Do not expect to feel any sort of pleasure, because it will destroy you. Do not hope for love, because you're not worthy of it. Those who love you will love you for the illusion of you, not for the real you. Do not hope that you will get anything out of life, because each passing year will take something from you. Do not even hope for anything as simple as a peaceful life, because you don't have a single reason to be at peace.

"Wish for work. There is little hope, given your sex,

that you will get far up the ladder, but perhaps you will serve your employer. Working will earn you money, which will give you no pleasure, but might be of some advantage to you—such as when it comes to marriage. Because you should not be so foolish as to suppose that anyone could want you for yourself.

"Apart from that, you can hope to live to a ripe old age, although that should be of little interest to you, and to live without dishonor, which is an end in itself. There ends the list of your legitimate hopes.

"Here begins the list of duties:

"You must be irreproachable, for the simple reason that that is the least you can be. Being irreproachable will have no other reward than being irreproachable, which must be neither a source of pride nor a pleasure.

"Not a moment of your life will be ungoverned by at least one of these duties. For example, even when you are in the bathroom for the humble purpose of relieving your bladder, you are constrained to ensure that no one will hear the trill of your stream. You should therefore flush continuously.

"If even these intimate and insignificant aspects of your existence are subject to commandments, remember what sort of constraints weigh on the truly important ones.

"Don't eat much, because you have to stay slim, not for the pleasure of seeing people turn to admire you in the street—they won't—but because it is shameful to be plump.

"It is your duty to be beautiful, though your beauty will afford you no joy. The only compliments you receive will be from Westerners, and we know how short they are on good taste. If you admire yourself in the mirror, let it be in fear and not delight, because the only thing that beauty will bring to you is terror of losing it. If you are pretty, you won't amount to much; if you are not, you will amount to nothing.

"It is your duty to marry, preferably before your twenty-fifth birthday, which is your date of expiration. Your husband will not love you, unless he's a half-wit, and there is no joy in being loved by a half-wit. You will never see him anyway. At two in the morning an exhausted—and often drunk—man will collapse in a heap onto the conjugal bed, which he will leave at six o'clock without a word.

"It is your duty to bear children, whom you will treat like gods until they turn three, when, with one clean blow, you will expel them from paradise and enlist them for military service, which lasts until they are eighteen, and then from twenty-five until death. You will bring into the world creatures that will be all the more miserable because during the first three years of their lives you imbued them with a notion of happiness.

"You think that's horrible? You are not the first to think that. People like you have been thinking that since 1960. And yet it has done little good. Some have rebelled, and you too may well rebel during the only free period of your life, between the ages of eighteen and twenty-five. The instant you turn twenty-five, you will realize that you are not married, and you will be ashamed. You will exchange your eccentric clothes for a tidy little blazer, white tights, and grotesque pumps. You will subject your magnificent glossy hair to excessive blow-drying, and you will feel relief when someone—a husband or an employer—wants anything whatever to do with you.

"In the unlikely event of your marrying for love, you will be even more miserable, because you will see your husband suffer. It is better not to love him. This will allow you to be indifferent to the collapse of his ideals (your husband may still have some even if you don't). For example, he has been permitted the illusion that he will be loved by a woman. He will quickly realize that you don't love him. How can you love someone when your heart is set in a plaster cast? You've been too weighed down by duties, too bound by limits, to be capable of love. If you love someone, you must have been badly brought up. For the first few days of your marriage, you will fake all sorts of things. It has to be said that no other woman in the world can fake quite the way you do.

"Your duty is to make sacrifices for others. But do not let yourself think that your sacrifices will make those for whom you make them happy. Those sacrifices will only allow them not to be ashamed of you. You have no hope of either being happy or of making others happy.

"And if by some extraordinary chance you manage to escape one of these prescriptions, do not take this to mean you have triumphed. Take it to mean that you must have gone wrong somewhere. Actually, you will very soon come to realize any illusion of victory can only ever be fleeting. Do not attempt to enjoy the moment. Leave that sort of error in judgment to Westerners. The moment means nothing, your life means nothing. No period of time less than ten thousand years counts for anything.

"If it is any consolation, no one considers you less intelligent than a man. If you are brilliant, everyone will know, even those who treat you like dirt. And yet, if you think about it, is that really so comforting? If they thought of you as inferior at least that would provide some explanation for the private hell in which you live, and offer you hope of escape—by demonstrating how wonderful your mind truly is. If you are seen as an equal, or even superior, your Gehenna, your living hell, is absurd. That means there is no way out.

"Ah, but there is one! Just one. One to which you have every right to avail yourself—unless you have been stupid enough to convert to Christianity. You have the right to commit suicide. Suicide is a very honorable act. Do not deceive yourself into believing that the hereafter will be anything like the jovial paradise Westerners describe. There's nothing like that on the other side. What makes suicide worthwhile is its effect on your posthumous reputation, which will be dazzling, a source of family pride. You will hold a cherished place in the family vault. And that is the highest honor any human being can hope to attain.

"Granted, you can choose not to commit suicide. But then, sooner or later, you will find you can no longer cope, and slip into some form or other of dishonor: take a lover, indulge gluttony, grow lazy. It has been observed that humans in general, and women in particular, find it hard to exist for any length of time without succumbing to one of these carnal pleasures. If we are wary, it will not be out of Puritanism. That is an American obsession.

"It is best to avoid any kind of physical pleasure, because it is apt to make you sweat. There is nothing more shameful than sweat. If you gobble up a steaming bowl of noodles, if you give in to sexual craving, if you spend the winter dozing in front of the fire, you will sweat. And no one will be in any doubt that you are coarse.

"The choice between sweat and suicide isn't a choice. Spilling one's blood is as admirable as spilling sweat is unspeakable. Take your life, and you will never sweat again. Your anxiety will be over for all eternity."

THE FATE OF the Japanese man isn't that much more enviable. Japanese women at least have the chance to leave the hell that is their work by getting married. Not working for a Japanese company, I began to see, might be an end in and of itself.

But the Japanese man has not been asphyxiated. He has not had all traces of his ideals destroyed from earliest childhood. He has been allowed to retain one of the most fundamental of human rights: that of dreaming and hoping. He has been allowed to conjure an imaginary world over which he is the master.

A Japanese woman does not have recourse to this if she

is well brought up—as is the case with the majority. Her imagination has been amputated. That is why I proclaim my profound admiration for any Japanese woman who has not committed suicide. Staying alive is an act of resistance and courage both selfless and sublime.

ALL THIS IS what I thought of when I contemplated Fubuki.

"What you are doing?" she asked me in an acerbic voice.

"I'm dreaming. Don't you ever do that?"

"Never."

I smiled. Mister Saito had just become the father of a second child, a son. One of the wonders of the Japanese language is that you can create an infinite number of names, drawn from all the parts of speech. By one of those bizarre quirks of which Japanese culture offers abundant examples, those who have no right to dream bear names that solicit dreaming, such as "Fubuki." Parents indulge in the most delicate lyricism when it comes to naming a girl. When it comes to naming a boy, on the other hand, the results are often hilariously mundane.

Thus, as it was perfectly acceptable to select a verb in

the infinitive as a name, Mister Saito had named his son Tsutomeru, which means "to work." The thought of a child burdened with an agenda disguised as a name was sadly funny.

I imagined the poor kid coming home from school in a few years, his mother waiting by the door. "So you're home, Work. Do your homework!" What if later he went on unemployment?

Fubuki was irreproachable. Her only flaw was that at age twenty-nine she still didn't have a husband. There was no doubt it was a source of shame to her. If a young woman as beautiful as she had not yet found a husband, it was precisely because she had so zealously applied the same supreme rule that served as a name for Mister Saito's son. For the last seven years she had submerged her entire existence in work. And successfully so, since she had achieved a professional standing rare for a woman.

Such devotion had made it absolutely impossible for her to wed. She could not, however, be reproached for working too hard because, in the eyes of the Japanese, you can never work too hard. There was therefore something contradictory in the rules laid down for women: irreproachable assiduity in their work habits meant that they might reach twenty-five without marrying and, consequently, make themselves open to reproach. The core of the system's sadism lay contained in this contradiction: obeying the rules eventually meant disobeying the rules.

I was fairly sure Fubuki was ashamed of being a spinster. She was too obsessed with perfection to permit the least omission in her compliance with the supreme instructions. I wondered whether she'd had casual lovers. Perhaps she had. What is beyond doubt is that she would never have flaunted jeopardizing her *nadeshiko*, her aura of virginity. Besides, given her schedule, I couldn't see how she would have even found the time for a banal affair.

I watched the way she behaved in the presence of an unmarried man—handsome or ugly, young or old, affable or loathsome, intelligent or dim-witted, it didn't matter, so long as he was not inferior to her in the corporate hierarchy of our company or his own. She would suddenly become so studiously sweet that it almost veered toward aggression. Hopelessly flustered, her hands fluttered toward her wide belt, nervously adjusting the buckle back around to the middle (her belt was too large for her tiny waist and tended to slip). Her voice became so tender it sounded like a sob.

I called this "Miss Mori's nuptial display." There was something nearly comic about watching her succumb to these antics, which I felt demeaned both her beauty and her position. There was something sad about it all, especially as the males for whose benefit she was deploying her seduction strategies didn't even seem to notice, and were therefore perfectly indifferent to them. I sometimes felt like shaking them and saying:

"How about showing a bit more chivalry? Can't you see all the trouble she's going to for you? Look, I know she's not doing herself any favors, but if you only knew how beautiful she is when she isn't trying so hard. Far too beautiful for you. You should weep with joy to be coveted by a pearl like her."

To Fubuki, I wanted to say:

"Stop it! Do you honestly believe this ridiculous performance is going to attract him? You're more seductive when you're treating me like a decaying fish. Pretend that he is me. Talk to him as if you were talking to me. Tell him that he's mentally unbalanced, worthless. At least you'd get a reaction."

There was also something I longed to whisper to her:

"Fubuki, wouldn't it be a thousand times better to stay unmarried than tie yourself down with some creep? What would you do with a husband like that? And how can you feel ashamed of not marrying one of these men, when you're so sublime, so Olympian? They're almost all shorter

76

than you. Don't you think that's a sign? You're too long a bow for any of these pathetic little shooters."

When an eligible bachelor had departed, my superior's face took less than a second to switch from simpering to stony coldness. Sometimes she'd look up and catch my mocking eye, then pinch her lips with hatred.

WORKING FOR ONE of the companies that did business with Yumimoto was a twenty-seven-year-old Dutchman named Piet Kramer. Although not Japanese, he had reached a level in the hierarchy equal to that of my fair torturer. As he was about six feet two, I thought that he was a potential match for Fubuki, and indeed, when he came to our office she threw herself into her nuptial display, frenetically twisting her belt backward and forward.

Kramer was a good man, and nice-looking. He was all the more suitable as a possible match because he was Dutch. Quasi-German origins made his membership in the white races less of a hindrance.

"You're lucky to work with Miss Mori. She's so kind!" he said to me one day.

This declaration amused me. I decided to make use of it by passing it along to Fubuki—with an ironic smile.

"That means he's in love with you," I added.

She looked at me in astonishment.

"Is that true?"

"Definitely," I assured her.

She was thoughtful for a few moments. This is what she must have been thinking: *She's white and she knows the white people's customs. I can trust her for once. But, whatever happens, she mustn't know.*

She affected indifference.

"He's too young for me."

"He's only two years younger than you. According to Japanese tradition that's the perfect gap for you to be an *anesan niôbô*."

Anesan niôbô means "older-sister wife." The Japanese think the ideal marriage involves a woman with slightly more experience than the man, so that she puts him at ease.

"I know, I know."

"In that case, what *is* wrong with him?"

She didn't reply. She seemed to go into a trance.

A few days later, Piet Kramer's arrival was announced. Fubuki was thrown into a state of panic.

It was terribly hot. The Dutchman had taken off his jacket and his shirt displayed gigantic rings of sweat under his armpits. I saw Fubuki's face change. She forced herself to speak normally, as if she hadn't noticed anything, but her words sounded unnatural because in order to get the

78

sound out of her throat she had to throw her head forward. The woman who was always so beautiful and so calm looked like a guinea fowl on the defensive.

While engaged in this pitiable spectacle, she was surreptitiously watching her colleagues, hoping against hope that they hadn't noticed anything. Alas, how could you tell if anyone had seen? More to the point, how could you tell if anyone Japanese had seen? The faces of Yumimoto's managerial staff expressed the impassive goodwill typical of meetings between two friendly companies.

The saddest part of it was that Piet Kramer hadn't noticed the commotion, nor had the slightest sense of the internal crisis agitating the kind Miss Mori. Her nostrils were palpitating. It wasn't difficult to guess why. She was trying to discern how far the Dutchman's axillary opprobrium extended.

It was then that the poor man unwittingly but fatally compromised his chance to contribute to the expansion of the Eurasian race. Seeing a blimp in the sky, he ran over to the bay window. The speed of his movement released into the surrounding atmosphere a fireworks display of olfactory particles, which were dispersed around the office by the draft created by his displacement. There was no doubt about it: Piet Kramer's sweat stank.

No one in the enormous office could have failed to

notice it. As for Kramer's boyish enthusiasm about the blimp, which was a commonplace sight, no one seemed to find it endearing.

By the time the malodorous foreigner left, my superior's face was drained of blood. Matrimonial hopes were about to deteriorate even further. Mister Saito made the first dig.

"I couldn't have stood it a minute longer!"

By saying this he had authorized everyone to malign their visitor. The others lost no time in making the most of it.

"Don't whites realize that they smell like corpses?"

"If we could only get them to realize how badly they stink, we'd have a fantastic market for really efficient deodorants in the West!"

"We might help them smell a bit better, but we can't stop them sweating. They're made like that."

"Even the women sweat."

They were ecstatically happy. The thought that what they were saying might upset me didn't occur to them. At first I was flattered. Perhaps they didn't think of me as white. I quickly set myself straight. If they were talking like this in front of me it was simply because I didn't count.

Not one of them guessed the significance of this episode for their colleague. Had no one noticed the Dutchman's armpits, she might still have deluded herself, closing her eyes (and nose) to this congenital defect in her potential fiancé.

She knew now that nothing would be possible with Piet Kramer. To have had the least contact with him would have been worse than losing her reputation; it would have meant losing face. She could count herself lucky that apart from me no one knew the designs she had had on the bachelor. And I didn't count.

Her head held high and her jaws clamped shut, she went back to work. From the terrible stiffness of her features, I could tell just how much hope she had placed in this man. And I had had something to do with it. I had encouraged her. Without my meddling, she might not have considered him seriously.

So if she was suffering, it was largely because of me. I should have taken pleasure in this. I took none.

TWO WEEKS AFTER I had left my position in accounting I committed my greatest blunder of all.

It had begun to seem as if I had again been forgotten about within the walls of the Yumimoto Corporation. This was the best thing that could have happened to me, and I was beginning to enjoy myself. From the unimaginable depths of my lack of ambition, I could conceive of no happier fate than sitting at my desk, contemplating the passage of seasons, and gazing upon the face of my superior. Serving tea and coffee, regularly throwing myself into the view out of the window, and not touching my calculator were all activities that more than fulfilled my fragile need to find a place within the organization.

After all, I deserved the situation I was in. I had gone to some trouble to prove to my superiors that my best intentions would not necessarily prevent me from being a disaster. Now they understood. Their unstated though universally approved policy was something along the lines of: "Don't let her do *anything* anymore!" And I had shown that I was up to these new expectations.

This sublimely fallow period could have lasted until the end of time, had I not committed that blunder.

One fine day we heard thunder in the distance. Mister Omochi was shouting. The rumbling came closer. We all started looking at each other apprehensively.

The door to the Accounting Department gave way like an outdated dam under the pressure of the vice-president's bulk surging in. He stopped in the middle of the room and howled like an ogre demanding lunch.

"FUBUKI-SAN!"

We knew then who was to be sacrificed to satisfy the appetite—worthy of Baal—of the Obese One. The few seconds of relief experienced by those temporarily spared were followed by a collective shiver of sincere empathy.

My superior immediately stood up and stiffened. She looked straight ahead, toward me therefore, but without seeing me. Magnificent as ever, she contained her terror and awaited her fate.

For a moment I thought Mister Omochi was going to take out a saber hidden between two rolls of fat and slice off her head. Had it fallen toward me I would have caught it and cherished it to the end of my days.

That cannot happen, I reasoned to myself. *Those methods belong to another age. He'll do what he usually does: summon this latest victim to his office and give her the dressing-down of the century.*

What he did was far worse. Perhaps he was in a more sadistic mood than usual. Perhaps it was because his victim was a woman, a very pretty woman. He did not give her the dressing-down of the century in his office. He did it right there, in front of the forty employees of the Accounting Department.

You could not imagine a more humiliating fate for any human being, and certainly not for a Japanese, and especially not for the proud and sublime Miss Mori, than this public pillorying. The monster wanted her to lose face; that was clear.

He approached her slowly, savoring the sway his destructive power held over her. Fubuki didn't move so much as an eyelash. She was more beautiful than ever. Then his fleshy lips began to quiver and he produced from them a volley of seemingly endless ranting.

Tokyoites have a tendency to speak at supersonic speed, particularly when they are telling someone off. The vice-president was also short-tempered and loose-jowled, and the combination of it all loaded his voice with such a scoria of fatty rage that I understood almost nothing of what he was actually saying.

However it did not require familiarity with the Japanese language to grasp the essential point: a terrible punishment was being inflicted upon a living creature, and it was happening a few steps from me. It was an abhorrent spectacle. I would have done anything to make him stop, but he did not stop—the supply of invective in his guts proved inexhaustible.

What crime could Fubuki have committed to deserve this? I never actually found out. I knew her abilities, her enthusiasm for work, and her professional demeanor, and they were all exceptional. Whatever wrongs she might have done had to have been venial. Even if they were not, the least Mister Omochi could have done was recognize how invaluable an employee this exceptional woman was, and temper his rage.

It was pointless to wonder what my superior's error might have been. Probably nothing for which she would have reproached herself. Mister Omochi was the boss. He was well within his rights, if he so wished, to use any pretext to sate his sadistic appetites on an employee. He didn't need a reason.

I was suddenly struck by what I was actually witnessing. He was raping Miss Mori, and if he had succumbed to this act of beastliness while being watched by forty people, the exhibitionism only amplified his pleasure. I wondered if someone that fat—he weighed at least three hundred pounds—was physically capable of having sex with a woman. As if in compensation, his bulk made him all the more potent at yelling, at making this beautiful creature's frail silhouette tremble not from passion but with terror.

I saw Fubuki's body yield. She had always held herself erect, a monument of pride. If her body was abandoning her, that was evidence enough of sexual assault. Her legs gave out. She slumped into her chair.

I can't have been the only one to realize the nature of

what was happening. I sensed profound discomfort in the others around us. They averted their eyes, concealing their shame behind their files or their computer screens.

At this stage, Fubuki was hunched over, her slender elbows resting on her desk, her tightly balled fists against her forehead. The vice-president's verbal machine gun shook her frail back at regular intervals.

I was somehow not sufficiently unwise to let myself do what, in other circumstances, would have been a normal reflex: to intervene. There is no doubt it would have aggravated the situation—for both the sacrificial lamb and for me. And yet I cannot pretend I felt proud of myself. Honor sometimes means doing something very unwise. Behaving like an idiot is better than dishonor. To this day I blush for having chosen sensible restraint over common decency. Someone should have done something; and since there was no chance the others would have put themselves at risk, it should have been me.

I know Fubuki would never have forgiven me for it, but she would have been wrong. The worst thing about the whole ghastly episode was the way the rest of us meekly watched, and did nothing. Our submission to absolute authority was abject.

It seemed to me that as time went on Mister Omochi's screams became more intense, proving, if further proof were even necessary, the hormonal element of the scene. His energy recharged tenfold by the spectacle of his own desire, the vice-president was becoming increasingly brutal. His shouting gathered strength, its physical impact overwhelming his victim.

Toward the end came a painfully poignant moment. Perhaps only I and Mister Omochi heard it—a frail voice, a child's voice.

"*Okoruna. Okoruna.*"

It was the plea a little girl would make to her enraged father.

"Don't be angry. Don't be angry."

This sad supplication was what a gazelle, torn to pieces and half devoured, might say to a lion, begging for its life. I knew this was a stunning departure from the dogma of submission, from the ban on defending oneself from anything that comes from above. Mister Omochi seemed a tiny bit disconcerted by this unfamiliar voice, but it didn't stop him. In fact, something about it seemed to give him greater satisfaction, and he began screaming even more loudly.

An eternity later, either because the monster had tired of his toy, or because this invigorating exercise had whetted his appetite for a double futon-mayonnaise sandwich, he left.

A deathly silence fell over the accounting department. No one except me dared look at Fubuki. She remained prostrate for a few minutes, then struggled to her feet and fled without saying a word.

I KNEW SHE had gone where women go when they have been raped—where there is flowing water, where you can be sick to your stomach, where you can be alone. In the offices of Yumimoto the place that best filled these requirements was the bathroom.

I simply had to go and comfort her. It was no good trying to reason with myself, or remember all the humiliations she had inflicted on me, the insults she had thrown in my face. My ridiculous compassion dictated. "Ridiculous" is the right word. It would have been a hundred times smarter to have intervened between Mister Omochi and my superior. That, at least, would have been courageous. Whereas what I did was thoughtless.

I ran to the women's room. She was standing in front of one of the sinks, crying. I don't think she saw me come in. Unfortunately, she did hear me speak.

"Fubuki, I'm so sorry. I'm with you with all my heart. I'm on your side."

I was already moving toward her, stretching out an arm that quivered with comforting intentions, when she turned to me with a look of incredulous anger.

Pathological fury made her voice unrecognizable.

"How dare you? How dare you?" she screamed.

I can't have been having one of my intelligent days. I tried to offer an explanation. I touched her arm.

"I didn't mean to upset you. I only wanted to . . . say I was your friend."

In a paroxysm of hatred, she threw off my arm so that it whirled like a turnstile.

"Will you be quiet? Will you leave?"

I stayed rooted to the spot, dumbfounded.

She walked toward me with Hiroshima in her right eye and Nagasaki in her left. Had she had the right to kill me, she would not have hesitated to exercise it.

I finally understood, and ran out of the bathroom.

BACK AT MY desk, I spent the rest of the day simulating busyness while analyzing my stupidity, vast subject for meditation that it was.

Fubuki had been humiliated from head to toe before her colleagues. The only thing she had been able to hide from us, the last bastion of honor she had been able to preserve, had been her tears. She had had the strength not to break down in front of us.

And I had gone and watched her cry. It was as if I had wanted to drink the final full measure of her shame. She could never have believed what I did was based on kindness, though misguided kindness.

An hour later, she sat back down at her desk. No one so much as looked at her. She, however, stared at me. Her dried eyes bored into me with hatred. I could read clearly what they were telling me: "You've got it coming to you."

Then she went back to work as if nothing had happened, leaving me to interpret at leisure my sentence.

It was clear she believed my behavior had been an act of pure revenge. I knew there was no doubt in her mind that my sole objective had been retaliation for the way she had mistreated me in the past, to pay her back for what she had done to me.

I longed to tell her she was wrong, to say, "Okay, it was stupid and thoughtless, but I beg you to believe me. I had no other motive than my good, well-meaning, and stupid humanity. Yes, it's true I resented what you did to me, but when I saw you being humiliated, all I felt was simple compassion. You're perceptive enough to know that no one in this entire company—no, on this entire planet—respects and admires you, holds you in such awe, as much as I do."

I will never know how she would have reacted had I actually said this to her.

THE FOLLOWING DAY. Fubuki greeted me with an expression of magisterial serenity.

She's recovered, she's feeling better, I thought.

"I've got a new assignment for you. Follow me," she announced in a controlled voice.

I followed her out of the room. I was already worried. My new appointment was not in the Accounting Department? Where was she taking me?

My apprehension grew sharply when I realized that we were heading for the bathroom. *It can't be*, I thought. We'll turn right or left at the last minute and head toward some office.

We veered neither to port nor to starboard. She was steering me into the bathroom. I told myself that she probably wanted someplace to talk about what happened yesterday. I was wrong.

"This is your new job," she declared in a calm voice.

With an assured expression of professionalism and efficiency, she informed me of my new task. My responsibilities were, as necessary, to replace the roll of "clean, dry toweling" when it had been used up, and to replenish the stock of toilet paper in each stall. She entrusted me with the precious keys to a storeroom in which these marvels were housed, safe from the covetous looks of the employees of the Yumimoto Corporation.

Then this delicate creature picked up a toilet brush and began to explain with convincing seriousness how it was to be used. I would never have imagined I would ever see the elegant Fubuki holding such an instrument, let alone pass it on to me as if it were a royal scepter.

Somehow, in my amazement, I managed to ask a question.

"Who am I taking this job over from?"

"From no one. The cleaning women come in at night."

"Have they handed in their resignations?"

"No, but you must have noticed that their nightly cleaning duties are not really enough. During the course of the day we often run out of towels, or discover that one of the toilet-paper rolls is empty, or even that one of the toilet bowls is stained. It's embarrassing, especially when we have people visiting from another company."

I asked myself which would be more embarrassing for an employee: to see a toilet bowl stained by one of their own, or stained by someone from another company. I didn't have the time to consider fully this question of etiquette because Fubuki evidently felt I had been told everything I needed to know.

"From now on, thanks to you, we will no longer endure any further inconvenience," she concluded with a sweet smile.

And she left. I was alone, dumbstruck, my arms hanging limply by my sides. The door opened again. It was Fubuki. Like an actor with a perfect sense of timing, she had returned to give me one last piece of information.

"I meant to tell you. Your work also includes the men's bathrooms."

LET ME RECAPITULATE. As a child, I had wanted to become God, then, having decided this was beyond my reach, I chose to become Jesus. Finally I settled on becoming a martyr.

As an adult, I renounced my religious ambitions, returned to the land of my early childhood, and looked for work as an interpreter in a Japanese company. Alas, that was too much to hope for. I was brought down a notch and became an accountant. But now there was no stopping the lightning speed of my decline. I was given the position of doing nothing at all. I should have guessed that nothing at all was still too good for me, for at last came my final assignment: lavatory attendant. My career was in the toilet.

This inexorable trajectory might have been cause for ecstasy. I'd heard it said that a singer whose range was so great that she could sing from soprano to contralto possessed an enormous talent. Well, I too had achieved that vast range—from heavenly choir to the sound of a toilet flushing.

Once my disbelief had subsided, I felt a strange sense of relief. I had lost the fear of falling any further.

FUBUKI'S THINKING COULD probably be summarized as follows: "You want to follow me to the bathroom? Fine. You can stay there."

I stayed.

Anyone else in my situation would have quit. But not if they were Japanese. Fubuki thought she had found a way of forcing me to resign, and hence lose face. Cleaning bathrooms was not deemed honorable in the eyes of the Japanese, but it was less dishonorable than losing face.

I had signed a year's contract, which expired on January 7th, 1991. It was now June. I would survive. I would do what a Japanese would have done.

By so doing I was not escaping the law that dictated that any foreigner wishing to integrate themselves into Japanese life must honor the customs of the empire. The inverse of this law does not hold true at all: those Japanese who take offense when outsiders fail to adhere to their code are unfazed by their own departures from other people's conventions.

I was conscious of this imbalance and yet bowed to it wholeheartedly. I wondered if it stemmed from my childhood. I had been awestruck by the beauty of my Japanese universe when I was young, and as an adult I continued to draw upon its emotional reservoir. The contemptuous horror of the system was stripped bare to me, and I saw repudiated that which I had most loved, yet I remained faithful to it. I did not lose face.

For seven months I maintained the bathrooms of the Yumimoto Corporation. Strangely, I did not feel as if I had hit rock bottom in my life. The job was far less anxiety-provoking than verifying expense reports. Forced to choose between working at a calculator and counting out rolls of toilet paper in the storeroom, I would have chosen the latter, without hesitation. Far better to convert the absence of paper into the presence of paper.

LAVATORY CLEANLINESS AND mental hygiene go hand in hand. To those who will inevitably find my submission shameful, I need to say that never, not once during those seven months, did I feel humiliated.

The moment that I accepted Fubuki's assignment, I entered into another dimension—a universe of pure derision. Reflexively, I knew that in order to cope during these seven months I would need to change my set of values. I had to turn my life upside down.

Through some mysterious process in my immune system, this reversal happened instantaneously. In a flash everything inside my head changed: dirty became clean, shame became glory, the torturer became the victim, and what was sordid became comic.

Let me emphasize the comic. The restroom period of my life was one of the funniest I have ever experienced— and there have been plenty of other funny periods. In the mornings, while the subway was carrying me toward Yumimoto headquarters, I already felt like laughing at what lay ahead for me on that day in my little kingdom. I had to struggle to stifle my hilarity.

Five women, myself included, worked in the Import-Export Division of the Yumimoto Corporation, and there were hundreds of men. Fubuki was the only woman to have reached managerial status. That left three other female employees, none of whom worked on this floor. My territory consisted only of the restrooms on the forty-fourth floor. Therefore the ladies' room was, so to speak, the private domain of my superior and myself.

Incidentally, my restriction to the forty-fourth floor proved—as if more proof were necessary—the perfect inanity of my appointment. If toilet-bowl stains (what those in the military so eloquently call "skid marks") were such an embarrassment for visitors, I didn't see how they could prove any less offensive in the bathrooms on the forty-third floor.

I didn't point this out. I would undoubtedly have been told that I was quite right. The bathrooms on that floor would have been added to my jurisdiction. No, I was content with the forty-fourth floor.

Not everything about my inversion of values existed purely in my mind. Fubuki was deeply humiliated by what she probably interpreted as my obtuseness and inertia. She had been banking on my quitting. By staying, I was calling her bluff. My dishonor was thrown right back into her lap.

This was never communicated in words. I did, however, have some proof of it.

One day I came across Mister Haneda in person in the men's room. This meeting made quite an impression on both of us: on me because it was difficult to imagine God in such a place; and on him because he was probably not aware of my new assignment.

After the tiniest hesitation he smiled, clearly thinking that, given my legendary kookiness, I had somehow gone into the wrong bathroom by mistake. He stopped smiling when he saw me remove the empty towel roll and replace it with a fresh one. He didn't dare look at me again.

I had thought this chance meeting might change things. Mister Haneda was too good a chairman to question the orders given by one of his subordinates, particularly if that subordinate were the only female manager in his division. Nevertheless, I had reason to believe that Fubuki was asked to explain what I was doing in there.

The next day, in the ladies' room, she spoke to me in a measured voice.

"If you have any grounds for complaint, speak to me about them."

"I haven't complained to anyone."

"You know very well what I mean."

Actually, I didn't know exactly what she meant. What should I have done to not look as if I were complaining? Run straight out of the bathroom to let Mister Hanada think I really had made a mistake?

98

Whatever the case, I loved the way my superior had put it—"If you have grounds for complaint . . ."—especially the "if."

Two other people were authorized to get me out of the bathrooms: Mister Omochi and Mister Saito.

It should go without saying that the vice-president couldn't have cared less what happened to me. Indeed, he seemed downright enthusiastic about my new assignment.

"It's good to have a job, isn't it?" he would say cheerfully, when we met in the bathroom, and without a trace of sarcasm. He probably believed that cleaning bathrooms would give me the fulfillment I needed, the kind of fulfillment that only honest work can provide. The fact that a creature as inept as myself had finally found its place in society was, in his eyes, a positive event. He must also have been relieved that he was no longer paying me to sit around doing nothing.

Had anyone pointed out to him that my position was humiliating, he would have exclaimed, "You think it beneath her dignity? She should count herself lucky for working for us!"

In Mister Saito's case things were very different. He seemed profoundly disturbed by this whole situation. I had begun to notice that he had grown terrified of Fubuki; she emanated forty times his power and authority. Nothing in the world would have given him the courage to impose his opinion.

When he came across me in the men's room, a nervous little grin crept over his sickly face. My superior had been right when she had insisted upon Mister Saito's humanity. He was good-hearted, if pusillanimous.

The most embarrassing moment came when I met Mister Tenshi. His face changed completely when he walked in the bathroom. After the first rush of surprise had passed, he turned orange.

"Amélie-san—" he whispered.

He stopped, realizing that there was nothing he could say. He walked straight back out, without having performed any of the functions for which the place was intended.

I never saw him there again. Mister Tenshi had found a way of manifesting his disapproval of my fate—by boycotting the rest rooms on the forty-fourth floor. He went to the forty-third floor. Angelic though he might be, he was still made of flesh and blood.

I soon realized that he had spread the good word to those around him; no one from Dairy Products used my men's room anymore. And I gradually noticed an increasing disaffection for it on the part of the other departments.

Bless Mister Tenshi. This boycott constituted a veritable revenge on Yumimoto. The employees who chose to relieve themselves on the forty-third floor wasted precious company time waiting for the elevator or taking the emergency stairs. In Japan, this is known as sabotage, and it is one of the most serious crimes one can commit, a crime so despicable that they use the French word for it. Only a foreigner could dream up a word for such base behavior.

This solidarity moved me. The word "boycott"—which originates from the name of an Irish landowner—suggests masculinity. And the blockade on my kingdom was exclusively masculine. There was no "girlcott." In fact, Fubuki seemed more fanatical than usual about using the rest rooms. She started to brush her teeth there twice a day; her hatred for me was having a beneficial effect on her oral and dental hygiene. She so resented me for not resigning that she would use any pretext she could to sneer.

Fubuki may have thought she was torturing me but in fact I was delighted to be given so many opportunities to admire her tempestuous beauty in this our own personal *gynaeceum*. No boudoir was ever more intimate than the women's room on the forty-fourth floor. When the door opened, I knew it had to be her, given, as I've said, that the other three female import-export employees worked on the forty-third floor. Our little space was like the stage for a play, a place for two tragic actors to meet several times a day to enact the next episode of their fight to the death.

GRADUALLY, THE DISAFFECTION for the men's bathroom on the forty-fourth floor became a little too flagrant. I hardly saw anyone there anymore—just one or two twits who didn't know better, plus of course the vice-president. I imagine that it was the latter who took offense at the situation and alerted the authorities.

My position must have posed a real tactical problem for the higher-ups: interventionist though they were, they could not actually force their employees to relieve themselves on their own floor rather than on the floor below. On the other hand, they could not tolerate this act of sabotage. They had to do something. But what?

Naturally, I was deemed responsible for their infamous behavior.

"This can't go on. You've disrupted everything around you once again," Fubuki told me one day in a fearsome voice.

"What have I done now?"

"You know very well."

"I swear that I don't."

"Haven't you noticed that the men no longer dare to use the bathroom on the forty-fourth floor? They're wasting time by using the one on the forty-third floor. Your presence here embarrasses them."

"I understand. But I didn't choose to be here. You know that."

"The insolence! If only you were capable of behaving in a dignified way, these things wouldn't happen."

I frowned.

"I can't see how my dignity fits in to all this."

"If you looked at the men who come to use the bathroom the same way you look at me, their attitude would be easily explained."

I burst out laughing.

"I don't look at them at all!"

"In that case, why are they so embarrassed?"

"It's quite normal. Just having a member of the opposite sex there is enough to intimidate them."

"And why do you not draw the obvious lesson from that observation?"

"What lesson would you have me draw?"

"Not to be there anymore!"

My face lit up.

"Are you relieving me of my men's room duties? Oh, thank you!"

"I didn't say that!"

"Then I don't understand."

"As soon as a man comes in, you go out. You wait until he's left before you go back in."

"Fine. But if I'm in the ladies' rest room, I won't be able to tell whether anyone's in the men's bathroom. Unless—"

"Unless what?"

I put on my most stupid, wide-eyed expression.

"I've got an idea! All we have to do is put a surveillance camera in the men's bathroom, and a monitor in the ladies' room. That way, I'll always know when I can go in there!"

Fubuki looked at me in consternation.

"A camera in the men's bathroom? Do you ever think before you speak?"

"Of course the men can't know they're being watched," I went on ingenuously.

"Be quiet! You're an idiot!"

"Let's hope so. Imagine if you'd given this job to an intelligent person!"

"What right do you have to answer me back like that?"

"What have I got to lose? It would be impossible to give me a more lowly position."

I'd gone too far. I thought Fubuki was having a coronary. She looked at me with daggers in her eyes.

"Be careful. You don't know what might happen."

104

"Tell me."

"I repeat: be careful. And find a way of not being in the men's bathroom when someone comes to use it."

She left. I wondered whether she was bluffing.

JUST IN CASE, I obeyed my new orders. Actually, I was relieved not to have to spend so much time in a place in which, during the space of two months, I had been given the distinct privilege of discovering that there was absolutely nothing refined about the bathroom habits of the Japanese male. Japanese women live in fear of making the least sound in a bathroom stall. Japanese men pay no attention to the subject whatsoever.

Even though I was spending less time in the men's room, I noted that employees from the Dairy Products Department had not resumed their use of the forty-fourth floor bathroom. Spurred on by their leader, their boycott continued.

Relieving oneself had become a political act.

Any man who still used the facilities on the forty-fourth floor was in effect saying: "My submission to authority is total and absolute, and I don't care if foreigners are humiliated. They don't belong at Yumimoto anyway."

Any man who refused might have expressed this opinion: "Respecting my superiors does not prevent me from being critical of some of their decisions. Furthermore, I think that we would benefit from putting foreigners in positions of responsibility in which they might be useful to us."

An ideological debate was raging at the Yumimoto Corporation.

EVERY EXISTENCE CONTAINS its primal trauma, an event dividing life into a before and an after, a trauma so great that even the most furtive memory of it is enough to make an individual freeze in irrational, incurable, animal terror.

The ladies' room had a lovely bay window. I spent hours standing before it, pressing my forehead against the glass, imagining again and again throwing myself into the view, letting the feeling of falling permeate my body until I was giddy. That is why I was never bored for one minute in my job.

I was right in the middle of a mental defenestration when a new drama erupted. The door opened behind me. It could only be Fubuki; and yet here was not the quick clean sound my torturer made when she opened the door. It was as if the door had been pushed in. The footsteps were not those made by her delicate pumps but heavy and thunderous, those of a yeti in rut.

Everything happened very quickly. I barely had time to turn around to see the great bulk of the vice-president bearing down on me.

Microseconds of astonishment were followed by an eternity of panic.

He grabbed me the way King Kong did Fay Wray and dragged me out into the corridor. I was like a doll in his hands. My terror peaked when I saw that he was taking me into the men's bathroom.

Fubuki's threats came back to me: "You don't know what could happen to you." She had not been bluffing. I was going to pay for my sins. My heart stopped beating. My mind composed a will.

I remember thinking he was going to rape me and kill me. I hoped that he would kill me first.

A man was washing his hands at one of the sinks, but the presence of a third party seemed to have no effect on Mister Omochi's evil designs. He opened the door to one of the cubicles and threw me onto the john.

I told myself my time had come.

He started yelling three syllables, over and over again, convulsively. So great was my terror that I didn't understand what they were. I thought they must have been the equivalent of the kamikazes' "banzai!" used very specifically for sexual assault.

He went on screaming these three sounds. Suddenly, the dim light of understanding dawned.

"NO PE-PA! NO PE-PA!"

Which meant in Japanese-American, "No paper! No paper!"

The vice-president was pointing out in his fashion that the toilet-paper roll had run out.

I leapt up and hurried off to the storeroom, then returned on my quaking legs, my arms laden with rolls of paper. Mister Omochi watched me install one in the appropriate place, shouted something that was presumably not a compliment, threw me out, and locked himself in the now fully equipped cubicle.

My heart in shreds, I took refuge in the ladies' room, crouched down in a corner, and started crying.

Fubuki chose that moment to come and brush her teeth. In the mirror I could see her, her mouth frothing with toothpaste, watching me weep. Her eyes were jubilant.

Just for a moment, I wished her dead. *Memento mori.*

I REMEMBER HAVING loved a Japanese film called *Merry Christmas, Mister Lawrence*, set during the Pacific War in about 1944, about a group of British soldiers in a Japanese POW camp. One of the Englishmen (played by David Bowie) and one of the Japanese officers (played by Ryuichi Sakamoto) formed what certain textbooks might call a "paradoxical relationship."

Perhaps because I was young at the time, I was completely overwhelmed by the film, especially by the scenes depicting the fraught interaction between the two heroes. The film ends with the Englishman being condemned to death by the Japanese officer.

Toward the end the Japanese officer comes to contemplate the Englishman, who has been buried up to his head, a form of execution that kills its victim either by exposure, hunger, or thirst. The British officer is barely alive by this point, his light-skinned complexion the color of a slightly blackened joint of beef. I was sixteen and it struck me that dying like that was a beautiful way of demonstrating one's love.

I couldn't help sensing a parallel between this story and my own tribulations in the Yumimoto Corporation. Of course there were huge differences, but I did feel like a prisoner of war, and my torturer was at least as beautiful as Ryuichi Sakamoto was handsome.

One day, while she was washing her hands, I asked Fubuki whether she had seen the film. She said she had.

"Did you like it?"

"The music was good. Too bad that the plot was so unrealistic."

(Perhaps without realizing it, Fubuki was guilty of the same "soft" revisionism afflicting so many young people in the Land of the Rising Sun. Her compatriots during the Second World War had nothing to be ashamed of, it went; their incursions into Asia were intended purely to protect the indigenous populations from the Nazis. I was not in a position to argue with her.)

"I think that you have to see the film as a metaphor."

"A metaphor for what?"

"For the relationships between people. For example, the one between you and me."

She looked at me, perplexed, wondering what sort of lame-brained idea I was entertaining.

"Yes," I went on. "There's the same difference between you and me as there is between Ryuichi Sakamoto and David Bowie. East and West. Behind the surface conflict lies reciprocated curiosity. Misunderstandings hide a genuine desire to understand one another."

However convincing I thought my argument, I realized that I had again gone too far.

"No," she replied.

"Why?"

I wondered which withering reply she might choose: "I'm not in the least bit curious about you"; or, "I have absolutely no desire to understand you"; or, "how dare you compare yourself to a prisoner of war!"; or, "there is something disturbing about the relationship between those two characters that I would have nothing to do with."

Instead, in a polite and neutral voice, she replied with an observation both clever and wounding:

"I don't think you look anything like David Bowie."

I had to admit she was right.

I SPOKE RARELY in my new post, not because it was forbidden but because an unwritten rule stopped me. When your job is as dreary as mine was, the only way of preserving your honor is by remaining silent.

If a bathroom attendant is chatty, people are likely to think she feels comfortable with her work, that she feels she belongs there, that she finds her job so fulfilling that she feels a desire to babble.

If, on the other hand, she remains mute, it is because she treats her work as monastic mortification; she is expiating the sins of humanity. The French Catholic writer Georges Bernanos and Hannah Arendt talk of the crushing banality of Evil; the bathroom attendant knows the crushing banality of dejection, a dejection that always remains the same however disgusting the superficial differences.

Her silence expresses her quiet desperation. She is the Carmelite of the rest rooms.

I was mute, therefore I thought.

I thought, for example, that despite the lack of physical resemblance between David Bowie and myself, what I had said to Fubuki about the film was true. The comparison held. Let's face it. For her to have condemned me to the life she had, her feelings toward me really couldn't have been what you might call normal. I was not the only person she despised at the Yumimoto Corporation. There were others she could have martyred. She had focused her cruelty on me alone.

I decided that I had been accorded a privilege.

READERS MIGHT THINK I had no life outside of Yumimoto. This was not the case. During this whole ordeal I was leading a life that was far from being either meaningless or insignificant.

I have nonetheless decided not to talk about that other life in these pages. First of all, my extra-Yumimoto existence is beside the point. Second, given the hours that I was working, my private life—though, I insist again, not insignificant—was kind of limited in terms of time.

Thirdly, most importantly—and a little schizophrenically—descriptions of my other life will not be found here because when I was stationed at my outpost in the bathrooms on the forty-fourth floor at Yumimoto corporate headquarters, scouring and scrubbing away, I simply found it impossible to believe that merely eleven subway stops away existed a place where people loved me and respected me, people who made no automatic connection between me and a toilet-bowl brush.

When these nocturnal and weekend elements of my life came to mind when I was working, they seemed like an illusion. *That house and those friends? An illusion. An invention.* What possible link could there be between my days and my nights? I thought of those photographs of towns flattened by bombs, showing wastelands of space with ruined, lifeless houses devoid of form—and yet whose commodes still stood, proudly open to the skies, perched defiantly on their miraculously intact plumbing. *When the Apocalypse comes, the only traces of human civilization to survive will be its porcelain monuments. My life is here alone, in these rest rooms on the forty-fourth floor. They are my world.*

People with menial jobs conjure up what Nietzsche

calls a background world, forcing themselves to believe in an earthly or heavenly paradise. Their mental Eden is as seductive as their job is repugnant.

I would walk over to the bay window and look down upon the eleven subway stops, trying to see that journey's end. But from there, no house was visible or even imaginable. *You see?* I told myself. *You only dreamed that life.*

Then, once again, I pressed my forehead against the glass, and once again imagined my trajectory through space. Throwing myself into the view outside of that window saved me.

There must be pieces of my body all over Tokyo to this very day.

THE MONTHS PASSED. Every day, the block of my time at Yumimoto was chipped away, though I had no sense whether it was happening quickly or slowly. My memory was beginning to work like a toilet bowl. I would flush it in the evening. A mental brush would eliminate the remains of the day.

This ritual cleaning served no real purpose, of course, since it was only smeared again the following day.

Most people know that bathrooms are conducive to monastic meditation; they are places designed for pondering. In the quiet of the rest rooms on the forty-fourth floor, I came to understand something profound about the country in which I was living: existence, in Japan, is an extension of The Company.

That is an observation already expounded upon in countless economic and sociological studies. However, there is a world of difference between reading a study and living the reality. I saw quite clearly exactly what this meant for the employees of the Yumimoto Corporation—and for myself.

My suffering was no worse than theirs; it was just more degrading. And yet I did not envy them. They were as miserable as I.

The accountants who spent ten hours a day copying out numbers were, to my mind, victims sacrificed on the altar of a divinity wholly bereft of either greatness or mystery. These humble creatures were devoting their entire lives to a reality beyond their grasp. In days gone by they might have at least believed there was some purpose to their servitude. Now they no longer had any illusions. They were giving up their lives for nothing, and they knew it.

Everyone knows that Japan has the highest suicide rate of any country in the world. What surprised me was that suicides were not more common.

What awaited these poor number-crunchers outside The Company? The obligatory beer with colleagues undergoing the same kind of gradual lobotomy, hours spent stuffed into an overcrowded subway, a dozing wife, exhausted children, sleep that sucked them down into it like the vortex of a flushing toilet, the occasional day off they never took full advantage of. Nothing that deserved to be called a life.

The worst part of it all was that they were considered lucky.

DECEMBER CAME. THE month of my resignation. The word "resignation" might come as a surprise. I was, after all, coming to the end of my one-year contract; it therefore should not have been a question of my having to resign. And yet it was. In a country in which until very recently, contract or no contract, you were always hired forever, you did not leave a job without following certain traditions.

To respect those tradition, I was to tender my resignation to every level of the hierarchy, starting at the bottom: first to Fubuki, then to Mister Saito, then to Mister Omochi, and finally to Mister Haneda.

I prepared myself for this duty. I was determined to observe the most important rule of all: not complain.

Moreover, my father had given me some firm instructions in the matter. He was concerned that nothing should threaten the good relations between Belgium and Japan. I was therefore not even remotely to suggest that any Yumimoto employee had mistreated me. Any motives for resignation—I would have to explain my reasons for wanting to leave such a promising position—were to be presented in the first person singular.

This did not leave me with much choice: I had to place full responsibility for leaving on myself. Still, I proceeded under the assumption that Yumimoto would be grateful if I helped them save face, and might even protest that I was being too hard on myself, and that despite it all I was a good person.

I requested an interview with my superior. Fubuki told me to meet her in an empty office at the end of the day. As I was about to meet her, a demon whispered in my ear: "Tell her that you can make more money working as a bathroom attendant somewhere else." I had difficulty resisting the temptation. In fact, I was on the brink of hysterical laughter when I was face to face with Miss Mori.

The demon came back. "Tell her you'll only stay if they charge anyone who uses the bathrooms fifty yen."

I bit the inside of my cheek. Stifling my laughter was such a consuming effort that at first I couldn't actually speak.

Fubuki sighed.

"Well? You wanted to tell me something?"

To hide my mouth's contortions, I lowered my head as much as possible, conferring upon me an apparent humility that must have delighted my superior.

"I am coming to the end of my contract and it is with very great regret that I announce that I cannot renew it."

My voice was meek and tremulous—that of the archetypal underling.

"Ah? And why is that?" she asked crisply.

I realized I wasn't the only one doing the acting. I followed her lead by reciting my prepared lines.

"The Yumimoto Corporation has offered me many wonderful opportunities to prove myself. I will be eternally grateful for that. Sadly, I have not proven myself worthy of the honor."

I again bit the inside of my cheek. Fubuki, on the other hand, had no trouble staying in character.

"Quite so. Why do you think you were not worthy?"

This took me by surprise. Was she really asking me

why I had not proven myself worthy of scrubbing toilets? Was her need to humiliate me really so great? Had even I underestimated her feelings toward me?

I composed myself, looked straight into her eyes, and took up her challenge.

"Because I do not have the intellectual capabilities."

I was deeply curious whether such grotesque submission would please her. Her expression remained impassive. It would have taken a highly sensitive seismograph to detect any tensing of the jaw. But I knew she was enjoying her part.

"I agree. Why do you think you lack these capabilities?"

"Because the Western brain is inferior to the Japanese brain."

Fubuki seemed both delighted by and prepared for this.

"That is certainly part of it. And yet we shouldn't exaggerate the inferiority of the average Western brain. Don't you think that this incapability derives primarily from a deficiency specific to your own brain?"

"Without a doubt."

"At first I thought that you intended to sabotage Yumimoto. Can you swear to me that you weren't being deliberately stupid?"

"I swear it."

"Are you aware of your handicap?"

"Yes. The Yumimoto Corporation has helped me to realize its existence."

Fubuki's expression remained impassive, but I could tell from her voice that her mouth was getting dry. I was making her deliriously happy.

"So the company has done you a great favor."

"I will be eternally grateful to it."

This somewhat surreal twist that our conversation was taking lifted Fubuki to unforeseen heights of ecstasy. Despite myself, I found it deeply moving.

I suddenly wanted to tell her how delighted I was at being the instrument of her pleasure. I wanted to tell her to be the snowstorm of her name, to bombard me with bitterly cold blasts of wind, flint-sharp icy rain. I accepted that I was a mortal lost in the mountains on which her clouds were unleashing their unmerciful fury.

Giving her such satisfaction cost me so little, and her need to torture me was so great. Looking into her eyes, I read signs of pure joy. How long I had been waiting to see in those eyes the smallest glimmer of pleasure.

"What do you plan to do next?" she asked simply.

I had no intention of telling her that I was doing some writing.

"Perhaps I could teach French," I replied blandly.

My superior burst into a scornful laugh.

"You think you're capable of teaching?!"

I realized that she wanted something more, so I instantly decided against telling her that I already had a teacher certification. I lowered my head.

"You're right. I still haven't understood my limitations."

"Obviously not. Tell me honestly what job you think you are capable of."

Ancient Japanese protocol stipulated that the Emperor be addressed with "fear and trembling." I've always loved the expression, which so perfectly describes the way actors in Samurai films speak to their leader, their voices tremulous with almost superhuman reverence.

So I put on the mask of terror and started to tremble. I looked into Fubuki's eyes.

"Perhaps ... I ... perhaps the garbage collectors would hire me."

"Yes!" she replied, a little too enthusiastically.

She took a deep breath. I had succeeded.

I THEN TENDERED my resignation to Mister Saito. He too arranged to meet me in an empty office but, unlike Fubuki, he seemed uncomfortable when I sat down opposite him.

"I am coming to the end of my contract and it is

with very great regret that I announce that I cannot renew it."

Mister Saito's face broke into a multitude of nervous
tics. As I was unable to interpret their meaning, I went on
with my lines.

"The Yumimoto Corporation has offered me many
wonderful opportunities to prove myself. I will be eternally
grateful for that. Sadly, I have not proven myself worthy
of the honor."

Mister Saito's body twitched convulsively. He looked
profoundly embarrassed.

"Amélie-san . . ."

His eyes searched every corner of the room, as if looking for the right words to say. I felt sorry for him.

"Saito-san?"

"I . . . we . . . I'm so sorry. I didn't want all this to happen."

A Japanese person genuinely apologizing happens about
once every century. I was horrified that Mister Saito should
have consented to such humiliation for my sake. It was all
the more unfair because he had had no part in my suc-
cessive demotions.

"Please don't apologize. Everything has happened for
the best. My time in your company has taught me a great
deal."

At least that was the truth.

"Do you have plans?" he asked me with a kind but appallingly tense smile.

"Don't worry about me. I'll find something."

Poor Mister Saito. I was the one comforting him. Despite his status and position, he was both a slave to and an inept torturer in a system that he almost certainly didn't like, but which—out of weakness and lack of imagination—he would never question.

IT WAS MISTER Omochi's turn. I was paralyzed with fear at the idea of being alone with him in his office. The vice-president, however, was in an excellent mood.

"Amélie-san!"

He pronounced my name in that wonderful and very Japanese way that somehow confirms a person's existence by throwing their name in the air.

He had spoken with his mouth full, but it was difficult to figure out what he was eating from the sound of his voice. It must have been gooey and sticky, the sort of thing it takes your tongue a long time to clean off your teeth. It didn't adhere to the roof of the mouth enough to be caramel. Too fatty to be liquorice. Too dense to be marshmallow. A mystery.

I threw myself into my well-rehearsed litany.

"I am coming to the end of my contract and it is with regret that I announce that I cannot renew it."

Whatever delicacy it was he was devouring was on his knee, hidden from me by the desk. He put a new portion of it into his mouth, but his fleshy fingers hid their cargo before I could see what color it was. That was maddening.

The Obsese One must have realized I was curious about what he was eating because he threw it on his desk. It looked like pale-green chocolate.

"Is that chocolate from the planet Mars?" I asked, perplexed.

He roared with laughter, then was convulsed with hiccups.

"Kassey no chokoreto! Kassey no chokoreto!"

This meant "Chocolate from Mars! Chocolate from Mars!"

I thought this was a pretty extraordinary way of greeting my resignation. His high-cholesterol hilarity was making me uncomfortable. I was suddenly worried he might have a heart attack right in front of me. How would I have explained it to the police? "I offered him my resignation and the shock must have killed him." No one at the Yumimoto Corporation would have believed that. I was the kind of employee whose departure could only ever be very welcome news.

No one would believe the green chocolate did him in. You don't die from chocolate, even if it is green. Murder was more likely. I would have had my share of motives.

In short, I had to hope that Mister Omochi didn't die, because I would have been the ideal suspect.

The typhoon of laughter finally ended, and I was about to deliver my second recitation when he interrupted me.

"It's melon-flavored white chocolate, a specialty from Hokkaido. Exquisite. They have perfectly re-created the taste of a Japanese melon. Here, try some."

"No, thank you."

I liked Japanese melon, but found the idea of it mixed with white chocolate repulsive.

For some reason my refusal irritated the vice-president. He asked again, in the form of a polite order.

"Meshiagatte kudasai."

Which means, "Please, do me the kindness of eating."

I refused again, as politely as I could.

He started to hurtle through the levels of language.

"Tabete."

Which means: "Eat."

I refused.

He shouted:

"*Taberu!*"

Which means: "Swallow it!"

I refused.

He exploded with rage.

"Now you listen to me! Until your contract is terminated you will obey my orders!"

"Mister Omochi, what difference does it make to you whether or not I eat some of this green chocolate?"

"Stop being insolent! It's not for you to ask me questions! You will do as I tell you!"

"What do I risk if I don't obey? Getting fired? That would be just fine."

Once again, after the fact, I realized that I had gone too far. A glance at Mister Omochi's expression told me that good relations between Belgium and Japan had come to a serious pass. His coronary now seemed imminent. So was my arrest.

"I'm so sorry."

He found enough breath to roar, "Swallow it!"

This was my punishment. Who would have believed that eating green chocolate would be a matter of international diplomacy?

I moved my hand toward the packet, thinking that this was perhaps what had happened in the Garden of Eden.

Eve had had absolutely no desire to bite into the apple, but a great fat serpent, in the grips of a sudden and inexplicable excess of sadism, had forced her to.

I broke off one of the greenish squares and brought it to my mouth. The color more than anything else was what had put me off. I put it in my mouth, bit into it, and to my great shame, discovered that its taste was far from unpleasant.

"It's delicious," I said grudgingly.

"Ha! Ha! Good, isn't it, this Martian chocolate?"

He was triumphant. International relations were back on an even keel.

Once I had swallowed the *casus belli*, I started into the next part of my recitation.

"The Yumimoto Corporation has offered me many wonderful opportunities to prove myself. I will be eternally grateful for that. Sadly, I have not proven myself worthy of the honor."

At first Mister Omochi was taken aback, probably because he had completely forgotten why I had come to talk to him; then he burst out laughing.

I had imagined that by debasing myself, so as to offer nothing for which they would have to reproach themselves, I would elicit polite protestations. Something along the lines of, "Yes, you were, Amélie-san, please. You were worthy."

This was the third time I had delivered my little resignation speech, and as yet there had still been no serious refutation. Far from disputing my deficiencies, Fubuki had made it clear that my case was more serious than even I had suggested. Mister Saito, embarrassed though he may have been, had not questioned the basis for my self-denigration. As for the Obese One, not only did he find nothing to contradict, he seemed to welcome my announcement with enthusiastic amusement.

I remembered a line from André Maurois: "Don't speak too ill of yourself. People will believe you."

Mister Omochi pulled a handkerchief out of his pocket, dried his tears of laughter, and, to my utter amazement, blew his nose. In Japan this is seen as the height of bad manners. Then he sighed.

"Amélie-san."

He said nothing more. I decided that he considered the matter closed. I stood up, said good-bye, and left.

THAT LEFT ONLY God.

I was never more Japanese than when I offered my resignation to Mister Haneda. My embarrassment was genuine, and expressed itself in a tense smile and stifled hiccups.

He greeted me with exceptional kindness in his huge and brightly lit office.

128

"I am coming to the end of my contract and it is with very great regret that I announce that I cannot renew it."

"Of course. I understand."

He was the first to react to my decision with any show of humanity.

"The Yumimoto Corporation has offered me many wonderful opportunities to prove myself. I will be eternally grateful for that. Sadly, I have not proven myself worthy of the honor."

He replied immediately.

"You know very well that what you say is not true. Your work with Mister Tenshi demonstrated that you have superb abilities in a field that suits you."

Now this was more like it.

He sighed.

"You've been unlucky. You came at the wrong moment. You're right to leave, but please remember that if someday you change your mind, you would be most welcome to return. I'm certainly not the only one who will miss you."

I knew he was the one who was wrong, but was moved nonetheless. He spoke with such persuasive goodness that for a fraction of a second I was almost sad at the thought of leaving the Yumimoto Corporation.

———

NEW YEAR'S: THREE days of rituals and compulsory rest. This kind of idleness is fairly traumatic for the Japanese.

For three days and three nights, they are not allowed to cook. They eat cold dishes, prepared in advance and stored in beautiful lacquered boxes. I used to love the *omochis*, a kind of rice cake, but that year I couldn't swallow a single one. When I brought one to my mouth, I was sure that it was going to roar "Amélie-san!" and burst into raucous laughter.

MY LAST DAY was January 7th, and after New Year's I went back for my final three days of work. The whole world was focused on what was happening in Kuwait. I had my eyes trained on the bay window; all I could think about was January 7th.

On the morning of the last day, I couldn't believe it had finally come. It felt as if I had been at Yumimoto for ten years.

I spent my day in the ladies' room on the forty-fourth floor in a mood of sanctimonious piety. I performed each tiny gesture with priestly solemnity. "In the Carmelite order," goes the phrase, "the first thirty years are the hardest." I almost regretted not being able to test the truth of that.

At six o'clock, having washed my hands, I went around the offices and shook the hands of those who had, in their various ways, let me know they thought of me as a human being. Fubuki's hand was not among them. I felt no rancor toward her. It was my self-respect that forced me not to say good-bye. I later thought that my attitude had been stupid. Choosing pride over any occasion to contemplate such an exceptional face was an error in judgment.

At six-thirty, I went back to my monastic cell. The bathroom was deserted. The neon lights didn't prevent my heart from feeling heavy. Seven months of my life—no, of my time on this planet—had been spent here. Not something to get nostalgic about. And yet I had a lump in my throat.

Instinctively, I walked over to the window and pressed my forehead against the glass. I knew that this was what I would miss most.

The glass stood between the glaring light and the velvet darkness of the outside world, between the cramped stalls and infinite space, between what was hygienic and what was truly pure. So long as there were windows, I thought, any human being could enjoy their small share of freedom.

I threw myself, one last time, into the view. I felt my body fall.

This final defenestration completed, I left the Yumi-moto Corporation, never to return again.

A FEW DAYS later, I went back to Europe.

On January 14th, 1991, I started writing a novel.

January 15th was the date of the American ultimatum to Iraq. On January 17th, war broke out.

On January 18th, Fubuki Mori turned thirty.

TIME, AS IT always does, passed.

In 1992, my first novel was published.

In 1993, I received a letter from Tokyo. Written in elegant Japanese characters, it read in its entirety as follows:

> AMÉLIE-SAN,
>
> CONGRATULATIONS.
>
> —MORI FUBUKI

The letter brought me great happiness.